# broken promises

## Port-Cartier Book 1

## mia elliot

# contents

# playlist

**Flume, Chet Faker** - Drop the Game
**Taylor Swift** - right where you left me
**Katy Perry** - The One That Got Away - Acoustic
**Hozier** - Like Real People Do
**The 1975** - Somebody Else
**Paramore** - Still Into You
**Taylor Swift** - This Love (Taylor's Version)
**Elvis Presley** - Can't Help Falling In Love
**Coldplay** - Yellow
**Lord Huron** - The Night We Met
**The Fray** - Look After You
**Ed Sheeran** - Perfect
**5 Seconds of Summer** - Ghost of You

# content warnings

This book is intended for audiences 18+. Should you have any specific questions about triggers, please don't hesitate to reach out to me at miaelliotauthor@gmail.com for more details. Your mental health matters.

**If any of the following elements make you uncomfortable, please proceed with caution:**

cheating - not between MCs
strong language
explicit sex scenes
injury of a parent - described on page

# Chapter 1
## Lucy

THE WORDS SWIRLED in front of my eyes, followed with a winky smile face that only stabbed at my heart further.

I blinked once as if the motion would magically make the words disappear, but they remained on my boyfriend's phone screen. My chest tightened as I dissected every letter in a simple text message.

"Jason, what's this?" I stammered. It felt like the phone was somehow contagious with his betrayal, yet I couldn't force myself to let go of it. My hands shook as I climbed out of bed and approached the door to our bathroom. "Jason!"

"What's what, babe?" Jason called from the shower. He had just finished his workout, and we were meant to head out for dinner together. Now, it felt like a cold water had been poured over me.

"You got a message from Luzzini's," I said. Luzzini's was a nearby Italian restaurant from which we often ordered pizza. There was no way they were asking him if he wanted to have some fun later. No, he was hiding someone's number from me.

The moment the words left my lips, Jason rushed outside. He'd barely had time to properly wrap a towel around his waist. He grabbed the smallest one, which looked ridiculous around his muscular frame, as he tried to keep himself covered, before reaching for his phone. I stepped back, still holding the device in my hand.

"Since when did they start texting you to ask if you want to have some fun later?" I asked. Just saying it out loud made me sick to my stomach. Bile rose to my throat, threatening to spill at any point now.

*This can't be happening.*

"Luce, I can explain…" His face was pleading as he took another step toward me.

"Go ahead. Explain."

His mouth opened and then closed again. For once, Jason was speechless as I stared at all 6'5" of him. His blue eyes were frantic, and strands of still-soaked blonde hair scattered over his forehead. The silence that followed was louder than anything he could have said.

"Who is she?"

"Look, I—"

"Who is she?!" I snapped. The back of my eyes burned, but I desperately tried to keep it under control. The last thing I wanted was to break into tears right now. He didn't deserve it. He didn't deserve *me.*

"I didn't want you to find out like this. There's really no easy way to say this, I suppose, but I want you to know that I didn't plan on anything like this happening. It just…did. You were so busy all the time, and we've barely been spending any time together. And I guess I've just…needed someone by my side. I needed to feel loved and appreciated." He swallowed, his entire body tense as he gathered the courage to say the words out loud. "What I'm trying to say is…I met someone else." He leaned against the bathroom counter, still trying to hold up the towel wrapped around him.

The urge to scream and cry was there, but neither of those things happened. My heart shattered into a million pieces, yet I remained surprisingly calm. I didn't know how I was doing it—all I knew was that I was taking the news well…all things considered. It seemed like disassociation went a long way. "And when were you planning to tell me any of this? How long has this been going on?"

He stayed silent, telling me it was longer than expected. I wasn't in the mood to play around. I needed to know how badly he had messed up so I could go through with damage control. "How long?" I repeated myself.

Silence.

"How long!?"

He flinched as I snapped, finally daring to meet my eyes again. "Jesus. I've been seeing her for six months! I didn't mean to; it just…happened. I was lonely, and she was there, and I…what are you doing?" he asked as I dashed out of the bathroom and into the bedroom.

"If you're lonely, you get a cat, Jason. You don't find someone else to stick your dick in," I told him, opening the closet we shared and nearly tearing the door out of its hinges. He followed closely behind, watching me grab the suitcase and pull it out.

"Please, can we talk about this? I can't—"

"I never would have cheated on you!" I snap at him, opening my underwear drawer and tossing a few panties into the suitcase. For all I knew, I was packing six pairs of underwear and nothing else. I just needed to get out of here. "This doesn't need to be said, but we're done. We're so fucking *done*," I swore. The tears threatened to spill down my cheeks at any point, so I tried to focus on the task ahead. I needed to pack my things as soon as possible.

I quickly rummaged through my shelves next, grabbing

only the most necessary items and throwing them in my suit-case. I'd come back for the rest of my things later—for now; I just wanted to be able to get through the next day or two.

Jason grasped my arm, turning me around so I'd face him. I couldn't even look at him.

"Babe, please, let's just talk about this. Don't make any rash decisions," he said softly. "Please, let's just talk all of this through. Let me explain myself."

"No. There's nothing to explain. Nothing you say is going to change my mind." My hands trembled more. I could barely grab the items I wanted to put in my suitcase. "You don't cheat on someone you love."

"Luce…"

"Don't!" I snapped at him. "Don't call me that. You don't get to call me that after what you've done." I zipped my suit-case up and quickly moved into the living room to grab my purse. I was on the verge of tears; I just needed to make it out before I let it happen. I'd be damned if I let him see me crying because of him. "I'll be back to pack up the rest of my stuff at some point."

A few more steps, and I was finally out of the door, slam-ming it shut behind me. Thankfully, he didn't try to follow me as I quickly made it to the car. I drew in a shaky breath as I popped the trunk open and put my suitcase in, not wasting a second before hopping in the driver's seat.

The moment I started the car, tears flooded my cheeks. My chest was tight, to the point where it felt like I couldn't breathe—to the point where it felt like I'd suffocate from this pain. This wasn't how things were meant to go. We built a life together, and our future was all planned out. Hell, we were planning to get a dog at some point soon. Who the hell cheated on the person they were planning to have a dog with?

Jason Blackwell, that was who.

Sure, I wasn't perfect, but neither was he. I had been busy

with teaching lately, but that didn't give him a pass to cheat on me because he was lonely. Being away from home so much sucked for me too—and somehow, I managed to refrain from finding someone else...someone more convenient.

A small sob left my lips as I tried to process everything that had happened in the past twenty minutes. I mean, I did decide I was leaving him the moment he admitted that he cheated with no proper plan.

I'd been through a breakup that broke me before, and I wasn't about to let myself go through the same thing again. Pulling up to the side of the road, I grabbed my phone and set a timer for five minutes.

Five minutes.

That was all I'd give myself today to cry and sob before I figured out my next move and found a way to move on. I watched as the clock started ticking down, second by second, counting down the time to the definite end of my relationship. I slammed my hand against the steering wheel, feeling more tears make their way down my cheeks.

How could this be happening to me?

I thought he was the one.

*And that's what you get for opening your heart up to someone again,* I cursed myself, my throat closing up. Every cell in my body hurt from not only the betrayal but also the grief of a life lost and left behind.

More sobs made it past my lips—the ugly ones that you can't control and that leave you heaving for air.

The five minutes I had given myself seemed to drag on forever, to the point where it didn't feel like I had any more tears left. When the last few seconds ticked away, I had nothing but soft sniffles left to give.

When my timer finally did buzz, I knew I needed to figure out where I was going to go. I could book a hotel room for the night, but the thought of being alone terrified me.

I needed to be not alone, at least not tonight. So, I called the only person I could count on right now.

I thought my fingers would have stopped shaking as I dialed my best friend, Sailor, but apparently not.

Sailor and I met during freshmen orientation and have been inseparable ever since. After our first year of college, we moved into an apartment and shared one until a year ago when Jason asked me to move in with him. Looking back, Sailor had been against it all along. And she was right. It was the biggest mistake of my life.

But still, I knew she'd have my back, no matter what, and she'd be able to be there for me. She worked from home for a graphic design company, so at least I wouldn't be left alone right now.

Sailor answered on the second ring, "What's up, girly-pop?"

"Hey." I suppressed another sob. "How would you feel about a roommate for a few weeks?"

Sailor sucked in a breath. She knew me better than I knew myself, so it wasn't surprising that she could instantly tell something was wrong. "What happened?"

"Let's just say that I wasn't the only person Jason was dating. I packed up my things and left—well, some of my things, anyway. I still need to go back and pick up everything I left behind, but I just…I couldn't stay there for a moment longer. I needed to get out. I didn't have a plan—"

"You don't even need to ask. Don't be ridiculous. And that asshole…he better pray I don't walk into him because there will be a price to pay. I can't believe it. The *audacity* this man has! Well, screw him! You're coming back home. Yes, of course, you can stay. You're welcome for as long as you need. I'll order pizza, and we can make margaritas. Then we can make voodoo dolls of Jason and stab his stupid face."

A small chuckle escaped my lips. "God, I love you."

"Of course you do. Now get your ass over here. And don't

ever ask me a stupid question like that again. You should've just come right to my door. My home is yours, too. It always will be."

I sniffled, relieved that I had somewhat of a plan. Not that I doubted her. "I'll be there in twenty minutes."

An hour later, I recounted the whole incident with Jason to Sailor, along with a pizza and several margaritas as she promised. I was on her cream sofa, surrounded by dozens of pillows, as she sat on the floor beside me, snagging another slice of pizza.

"You can't go back there under any circumstances. I'm more than happy to go and pick up your things if you need me to," she said, brushing her blonde hair behind her shoulders. Her brown eyes remained glued to me. "You're welcome to stay here for as long as you'd like...but do you know what's your move now?"

"Thank you," I said softly, leaning back against the fluffy sofa. "I appreciate you letting me stay here. I'm going to start looking for a new place soon. Lucky for me, it's summer break from teaching, so that's one less headache." I sighed. "And, of course, I have to break the news to my mom."

Sailor munched on her pizza. "Oh, Eve's going to be fine with it. Don't you worry." She and my mom were on a first-name basis. They met a few times during the time we shared an apartment and have adored each other ever since. My mom considered Sailor her second daughter.

"I'm not too worried about that. My mom's always been cool with my choices. It's just..." I trailed off. "I think she may push for me to move back home."

"Well...." Sailor dragged the word out. "You know, that

might not be the worst idea," she suggested between bites. "I mean, you do need a fresh start, and you need to be as far from that asshole as possible."

"What, moving?" I raised my eyebrow. "Love you too, babe."

Sailor laughed. "You know I love you, and you know I'd love nothing more than for you to spend the rest of your life by my side...but maybe taking a little vacation to see your mom could be the right way to go about it. Clear your mind, get out of the city for a bit..." She leaned up to nudge me. "You'll have fun."

"I don't know," I debated. "It's been a decade since I last visited. Not since high school graduation. Mom's always been the one hopping on planes to come here." And for a good reason. The heartbreak that I endured back then left me scarred for life.

"I get it, but a change of scenery might do wonders for you. Just think about it," she urged, her eyes reflecting genuine concern. And her words were getting through to me. Maybe I was crazy, but for once, I *was* actually considering it.

"I'll think about it," I conceded. The idea of escaping the city, even if I would inevitably run into my now ex-boyfriend, sounded good right now. Out of the two, Luke was currently the lesser evil.

# Chapter 2
## Lucy

THE FOLLOWING DAY, when Sailor locked herself in her office for her round of online meetings, I figured I had some time to decide my next move. Sailor's words last night got through me. Seriously, I spent years avoiding Port-Cartier, and over what? Over a breakup that happened an eternity ago?

I missed my mom, and I know she missed me, too. If there was ever a time to visit, it was now. Before I could change my mind, I grabbed my phone, dialing my mom's number as I faced the window overlooking the city. Green trees extended through the park that her window overlooked, the leaves dancing in the soft breeze.

"Hey, sweetie," Mom answered, excited to hear my voice. "How are you? I didn't expect your call today."

I bit my lower lip, silent momentarily as I summoned my courage. "Well, I have a change of address. I figured you should know."

"What do you mean? Is everything all right?"

"Not...exactly. Jason and I broke up." I closed my eyes to fend off the threat of tears. I wasn't doing this right now. I intended to keep all the tears during the five-minute confinement I had yesterday. He wasn't worth a single more tear. "He cheated on me."

"Oh, Luce. I'm so sorry. I wish I could give you a big hug right now."

*Me too,* I thought to myself. Only a chosen few called me Luce, and my mom was one of them.

"Thanks, Mom," I said, a solitary tear escaping my eye. *Stupid Jason.* I quickly wiped it away. "It is what it is, I guess. I just wanted you to know."

On the other side of the line, my mom remained silent for a moment. "Well, why don't you come home to visit, honey? God knows I miss my girl. And it's summer break for you, so you're not tied down with work."

The suggestion prompted more tears to fall. This time, it wasn't about Jason. It was about me missing my mom. "I miss you too. Sailor suggested the same thing."

"Of course she did," my mom remarked with a chuckle. "We're one mind in two bodies. And we're both telling you this is a good idea, so you better listen. So, what do you say?"

Every cell in my body protested at the thought. That was the aftermath of avoiding this trip for as long as I could remember. But it was a time for change—I knew it. "You know, I could use a vacation."

"It's settled then. I'll book your ticket. Just let me know when, and I'll make it happen."

I laughed once more. "Mom, I can pay for my ticket."

I was met with a low *tsk* sound. "Let me take care of my baby." I knew my mother well—she wouldn't relent. My mom was known for her stubborn streak something she passed down to me.

"Fine," I grumbled, practically hearing her clap in the background. I guess this was happening.

"Okay, I'll book it and send you the details. I can't wait, Luce. You're going to have the best time. A lot has changed since you left."

It might have, but some scars within me remained the same.

# Chapter 3
## Lucy

ONE WEEK LATER, I scanned the arrivals area for my mom, but I couldn't spot her. In a not-so-surprising twist, my mom had only booked me a one-way ticket, assuring me it was to grant me the freedom of an open-ended stay. So, why couldn't I shake the suspicion that my mom secretly hoped I'd decide never to return?

*Ah, that's right.* It was because Eve was always a woman with an agenda.

Around me, people moved back and forth—some arriving, some departing, and others waiting for their loved ones. And my mom was *still* nowhere to be found. Pulling out my phone, I dialed her number. It rang once before she picked up.

"Hey Mom, where are you?" I looked around. "I'm at the exit and can't find you..."

"What do you mean?" she questioned. *No*, this wasn't happening. She couldn't have forgotten about this.

"I just landed. I thought you were going to pick me up and—"

In the middle of my words, a police cruiser rolled up before me. An older man lowered the window and said, "Are you Lucy Milburne?" My knees went weak as I stared at the man with salt-and-pepper hair and warm blue eyes. He didn't seem like he was there to arrest me, but why would he be there in the first place?

"Yes…" I answered slowly.

"Surprise!" Mom yelled into the phone, making me jolt. From my initial shock of a police car pulling up in front of me, I had forgotten that I had been on the phone with her.

"What's the surprise, exactly?" I questioned, still splitting my attention between my mom and the police officer.

"I got you an escort for your ride home," she responded. My mouth gaped open. I, for once, was speechless.

"Don't you think the police have more important things to do than to drive around someone who's just landed?"

My mom laughed on the other side of the phone. "Oh, pumpkin, Edward is a good friend of mine. He offered his help. I'm very busy at the flower shop, so I accepted his offer. I hope that's okay."

"Of course," I responded. I couldn't have expected her to drop her life for me, but it would've been nice if she picked me up. At least this one time. "I'll see you at home."

As I hung up, the older police officer—whose name I now knew was Edward—grabbed my luggage and stowed it away in the trunk before opening the door so I could get in the car.

"I get to sit in the front seat?" I asked him, getting in.

"Well, you're not under arrest, so that's fine." He settled on the driver's seat, flashing me another smile. "Most people call me Ed. I was only Edward when my wife was angry at me," he explained as he started the car.

"I'm Lucy, but you already know that," I replied. "How do you know my mom?"

"Eve is a good person. I moved to Port-Cartier after my wife died eight years ago. She helped me find a place and get settled. Your mom was one of the first friends I made here." As I listened to Ed's story, my gaze wandered around the familiar landscapes as we headed to the town. Beautiful mountains rose in the background, with the ocean extending as far as my sight could reach to my left.

"I'm sorry about your wife," I expressed my condolences, but Ed smiled again.

"It's okay. It was a long time ago. Eve told me the other day that you were coming home and asked if I would give you a hometown welcome. It's the least I could do, especially after everything you've been through…"

I sighed, sinking into my seat. The concept of privacy was foreign to my mom. Even when I was a teenager she made sure half the town knew that I had gotten my period the first time.

"I'm sorry about your boyfriend. He sounds like a douche-canoe."

The words caught me off guard, and I burst out laughing. "You know what? He *is* a

douche-canoe. Thank you."

The rest of the drive from Rockwood was in a comfortable silence. As we approached Port-Cartier, memories flooded my senses. I had spent a good portion of my life here, and not much seemed to have changed. Exposed brick buildings and colorful houses, with luscious trees scattered in between. Tiny shops and restaurants piled alongside the road, ready to welcome customers. Everyone was in their element, chatting with those around them, laughing, making sales. Not a single soul would notice someone who had just returned home. And it was better that way.

My gaze drifted toward the small one-screen movie theater and a diner beside it. Both were, to my surprise, still open. My heart clutched at the sight, and my mind welcomed unwanted memories, hitting me with a wave of nostalgia.

*The illuminated sign flickered above us, casting a pink glow. Luke intertwined his fingers with mine, giving me a small smile. My heart fluttered at the sight, especially as his hand locked tighter around mine.*

*"What do you want to watch tonight?"* he asked me. His brown hair sat wildly around his face, matching his soft blue eyes. I would never get enough of the way he looked at me. I smiled.

*"You know there's only one movie playing, right?"* I asked him. *"And it's a chick flick, which I doubt you'd want to watch anyway."*

*"If you want to watch a later movie…we can grab some dinner beforehand. But I'll watch whatever you want to watch,"* he assured me, drawing me in closer. His other hand rested on my hip.

*"Even a chick flick?"*

*"Even a chick flick,"* he confirmed.

*"Why?"*

*"Because I love you, Luce."* The words caught me off guard entirely. I stared at him, my mouth gaping open just a little bit. We'd only been dating for six months—I didn't expect him to say the words so soon. Yet, I was entirely certain I felt the same way.

*"I love you, too."*

"We're almost here." Ed's voice snapped me out of my memory. He flicked on the

sirens of the police cruiser. The sudden noise made me flinch in my seat, my eyes bugging from my head.

"What are you doing?" I shrieked, looking around frantically. "Is there a crime in progress?"

"Nope, just giving you a welcome home." Ed grinned. "As I said I would."

"Oh my God, turn those off, please!" I yelled over the sirens. My cheeks burned in embarrassment as the bystanders started looking around, thinking something was happening.

"No can do. Not until we turn into the driveway," he chuckled. "I promised your mom I would use the sirens, and you know I've got to keep my promise to Eve."

I shrank in my seat, praying for the earth to open up and swallow me whole. This was *not* how I wanted to arrive in town—this much attention could never be a good thing, especially when one has just made a return to their hometown.

As the cop car pulled into the driveway, I caught sight of

my childhood home. It was just as I remembered it—a beautiful wrap-around porch adorned with peonies of every color. Mom had always had a knack for gardening, which made sense since she ran the town's famous floral shop. A sense of comfort washed over me as I hopped out of the

car, eager to escape the incessant sirens. Ed turned off the sirens and opened his door,

joining me on the lawn. Mom appeared at the front porch, arms open wide in

excitement. Everyone always said we looked *just* the same. The same black hair, the same emerald, green eyes. Her face had two extra decades' worth of wrinkles compared to mine.

"Luce!" she exclaimed, engulfing me in a warm hug. She didn't release me for a few seconds until I finally managed to squirm away. "I've missed you, sweet girl."

"I missed you too, Mom," I admitted. Behind us, Ed had already retrieved my suitcases, plopping them on the front porch.

"Let's go inside and catch up. Ed, would you like some of my lavender iced tea? I just brewed a fresh batch," my mom said. A wide smile spread across his lips.

"You know I can't say no to your tea, but only if I'm not interrupting anything..." Ed hesitated. My mom waved her hand at him.

"Oh, nonsense. You're not interrupting anything at all."

We walked up the front steps together, our arms intertwined. As we approached the

front door, I reached out to open it. As soon as I stepped inside, a chorus of "Surprise!"

echoed from all directions. My eyes widened as I took in the scene before me. Familiar

faces filled the room—even my Kindergarten teacher, Ms. Penny, was there. Confused, I

turned to my mom for an explanation.

"What's going on?" I asked but forced myself to put a smile on, nonetheless. This was precisely what I didn't want. I came here for peace and quiet—to recharge and sort out my head. I wanted to spend some time with my mom and wander around the town, and my trip was already off to an unexpected start.

I appreciated my mom's effort, but I had to fight the surge of panic that spread through me.

"I thought we could have a little welcome home party with some of the town," my mom explained, pushing me inside. As I did, I noticed more balloons and a massive cake— as if I was celebrating a birthday rather than returning home.

For the next hour, I made small talk and explained to everyone why I was back home. This wasn't what I expected, so I quickly came up with the first lie that came to my mind. Instead of telling everyone I had been cheated on, I explained I was here for my summer break because I wanted a short break from Seattle. Everyone seemed to buy the lie.

So far, so good, I thought to myself, until my eyes set on the bluest eyes I have ever seen.

It was him. Luke.

# Chapter 4
## Luke

WHEN MY MOM told me that Lucy's mom announced that Lucy was coming back, I couldn't believe it. At first, I thought I had misheard her—there was no way Luce would have returned to Port-Cartier willingly. Not after our breakup ten years ago.

I didn't want to break her heart, but I knew that was for the best. I *knew* her. I knew she would've gladly sacrificed her dream by following me to college. I had been selfish many times in the past, but it was one time I couldn't allow myself to do it. I loved her too much.

So, we went our separate ways.

I went to college a few states away and returned home to take over my dad's ship-building business, and she vanished into thin air—until now.

"And guess what," my mother beamed. "Eve invited us to the welcome home party, too." I was sure Lucy had no idea about any of it for two reasons—first, she wasn't big on surprises, and secondly, I was the last person she would have invited to come.

I was running twenty minutes late—mainly because I questioned whether it was a good idea to go to the party in the first place. At last, my decision was made, and I found myself knocking on the navy-blue door with a bouquet in my hand.

Was it too much? Maybe. But after being gone for ten years, I felt like I couldn't come to see her with empty hands.

I held my breath as I waited for the door to open, expecting to see the only girl I had ever loved…until Eve popped up at the door with her trademark, dashing smile.

"Luke! How good to see you. Come on in," she prompted me, practically dragging me inside. I stumbled inside, looking around nervously. Only then did it hit me that she was *in* here somewhere. "Luce's in the back. I'll go get her."

"That's all right, Ms. Milburne. I'll find her myself."

Finally remembering to move my feet again, I made my way through the crowd, searching for her. She was in the kitchen, surrounded by some childhood friends who seemed eager to hear about her life in the big city.

I exhaled softly. She was just as beautiful as I remembered. Her dark locks cascaded down her shoulders effortlessly, framing her oval face. Her smile on her face was enough to light up a room, but it didn't reach her green eyes. I was right —she didn't want this party.

And more importantly, she made me feel exactly how I did all those years. My stomach twisted with regret. I shouldn't have let her go all those years ago. I should have found a way to make it all work. I was now sure that a man only got to meet that kind of a woman once in his lifetime. Sure, I dated here and there, but none of my relationships were serious. Now I fully understood why—because none of them compared to *her.*

We were young when we dated—so young that many would tell us we didn't even know what true love was, but I knew that wasn't the case, because the impact she left on me shaped me for life.

I didn't even realize we were staring at each other from

across the room until she moved first, heading upstairs. I clutched the flowers in my hand, giving her a few moments of a head start before I followed her to the bathroom.

I wasn't sure whether she was avoiding me or if it was just a coincidence, but I knew we had to talk, especially if she would stay in town. I didn't want us to find ourselves in awkward situations in public.

I shifted from foot to foot as I waited for her in front of the bathroom. Each second dragged out to an eternity—until she finally opened the door, nearly bumping into me.

"God!" she exclaimed, stumbling backwards as she brought her hand to her chest. "You scared the shit out of me."

"I'm sorry," I quickly apologized. That was the last thing I wanted. I stalled, unsure whether I should go in for a hug.

*It's probably too soon,* I told myself, extending my hand that still held the flowers toward her.

She arched her brow but took the flowers, nonetheless. It was a beautiful bouquet with her favorites—peonies and baby breath. "Flowers from my mom's flower shop, Luke?"

I shrugged my shoulders. "Well...it's not my fault she has the best flowers in town," I admitted. And there was no way I was getting her anything less than perfection. When she didn't respond, I quickly continued, "It's good to see you, Luce. To be honest with you, I still can't fully believe you're back."

"I can't either, but here I am," she muttered. I didn't miss the stiffness in her body as she talked to me. It broke my heart, but it was understandable. We hadn't spoken since the night I broke up with her. "Thank you for the flowers..." she murmured before taking a step to walk away.

*No.* This wasn't how our first conversation after all those years would end. I needed to talk to her a little longer.

"Luce, why did you come back?" I blurted out the first thing I could think of. She turned around in a heartbeat, staring at me with those green eyes that had the power to disassemble every bit of rational thinking in my brain.

*God, she's still so beautiful. How could I have ever let her go?*

"I mean, I'm not complaining. I'm glad that you're back… I'm just curious about what changed your mind after all these years." The first few years after she left, her mother tried to convince her to come to Port-Cartier over the holidays, but she refused every time. What changed? Was it something in her personal life? Did she come to plan her wedding with her mom?

My heart clenched just at the thought of her with another man. Logically, I knew she must have had a fair share of relationships over the past decade, but it didn't make the image in my mind any easier to stomach.

"I needed a change for a little while. I wanted to leave Seattle over the summer, and my mom invited me to come over. I figured it was about time I accepted her offer," she explained. There was still a certain dismissiveness, a certain coldness to her tone. And I deserved every bit of it.

I slung my hands into the pockets of my jeans. "How do you like Seattle? In comparison to Port-Cartier, I mean. I've never had a chance to ask you."

"Seattle is fine. You get used to it after a while. It's a place like any other." She didn't sound like she had made a home out of it. I understood it all too well. I spent my entire life in Port-Cartier, yet after she left, it never felt like home like it used to.

"I can't imagine myself living in a big city like that. It would probably be a little too busy for my liking," I said. I had a nagging feeling that she was eager to end this conversation, while I wanted to keep it going for the rest of the night. How did I go for a decade without talking to her? Now that she was back, feelings flooded me all over again, and all I could think about was how much I missed her all along. "Are you…seeing someone?"

"Excuse me?" She stared at me in disbelief.

"Sorry, I just...I'm just wondering. Are you seeing anyone?" I didn't have the right to ask the question, but it found its way to my mouth regardless. I needed to know.

"I don't see how that's any of your business," she said firmly. Her eyes remained locked on mine to the point where I could barely focus on anything else. My heart thudded inside my chest, wanting to fight its way out and head back home to her. "But if you have to know, I just ended things with someone."

So that was the reason she came back. She was heartbroken. A surge of anger rushed through me—how could anyone have shattered her heart? I wanted to ask more questions... until I remembered that I did the exact same thing once upon a time. The realization shut me up, especially as she pressed her full lips into a thin line.

"If you'll excuse me, I need to go unpack. It was good seeing you, Luke," she said, retreating down the hall to the room I recognized as her bedroom from a decade ago. I was sure of three things as she shut the door behind herself, with my flowers still in her hand.

One, Lucy still had the same hold on me as she had ten years ago.

Two, I wanted to help heal her broken heart.

And three, I had a new chance to win her over, and I wasn't going to mess it up.

# Chapter 5

## Lucy

A KNOCK SOUNDED *at my window as I read on my bed. It was a book I needed to read for my English class, but my focus was anywhere but on the letters in front of me. A small smile curved my lips as the sound softly echoed through my room. I knew* exactly *who was knocking on my window. Luke was trying not to wake up my mom.*

*And for a good reason. She would've been pissed off at both of us, and I'd be grounded. Slowly sneaking over to my window, I pushed the glass away from the wooden frame, opening it for him.*

*"What are you doing here?" I asked Luke as I took him in. He was in his usual attire—jeans and a sweatshirt. It was a favorite of mine, one that I had tried to steal many times. So far, my mission had been unsuccessful.*

*"I wanted to see you. I missed you," he spoke in a low, hushed tone.*

*I laughed. "I just saw you an hour ago, Luke. Don't be dramatic."*

*"That's an hour too long," he retorted. "Can I come in?"*

*I bit my lip. Luke had been in my room before, but not after my mom had gone to bed*

*and certainly not with the door closed. It was one of the rules she had set for her sixteen-year-old daughter, even if I did behave decently. Luke was allowed to come over, but I had to keep the door open.*

*I considered my options for a moment longer, and then nodded.*

*"Sure, but you need to keep quiet. If my mom finds out you're in here, I'm dead." Well, I'd be grounded, but that was about the same thing if you wanted to survive high school. I stepped aside, watching Luke climb up the massive oak tree by my window before he hopped into my room.*

*I stood there awkwardly. I didn't know what to do with him in my room at night, particularly without my mom's knowledge. Luke hugged me, placing a soft kiss on the top of my head. "God, you smell good, Luce," he murmured as he inhaled a lung full of my scent.*

*"Well, I did just have a shower, so you're just in time if you want to make it here when I smell good," I teased him, cringing inwardly. God, why was I so nervous? We hadn't had sex yet, but we were getting close. I knew he was ready, but I wasn't. He wouldn't try to talk me into something I wasn't prepared for, but this was foreign and nerve-wracking, regardless. "Come here," I added, taking his hand and tugging him into my bed. His broad arms wrapped around me, holding me in a tight hug as sleep slowly lulled me in. All I knew was I wanted to stay here forever.*

*"Luce, are you up?" My mom's voice suddenly rang out, snapping me out of the blissful slumber I had been in for the past...well, however many hours. I quickly sat up, feeling my heart sink into my chest.*

*"Shit!" I put a hand over Luke's mouth. He had woken up when Mom had called out. He licked my palm with a mischievous look on his face while I was a bundle of panic and anxiety, terrified that my mom would catch us. If she did catch us I didn't want to know what her punishment would be.*

*"Are you up?"*

*"Yes...yes." I wasn't. I forgot to set my alarm. I quickly hopped out of bed, grabbing whatever clothes were within my reach.*

*"Okay, well, Luke will be here in fifteen minutes to pick you up, so don't keep him waiting."*

*Luke now also sat up in bed, looking at me with a smirk. "Should I tell her I'm already here?" he asked, and I swatted at his stomach in another wave of panic.*

*"You need to go!" I told him. Luke laughed as he climbed out of the window, and I was just thankful I avoided getting caught…but that didn't help with the rush I was trapped in for the morning.*

*I was going to be late.*

My bedroom was exactly as I had left it. The boy band posters still clung to the pale purple walls. My bed was covered in floral bedding I recall from my teenage years, and all my knickknacks were left in their place. It was like I was stepping back in time.

And all I could think about was him.

God, he looked good. Ten years had done wonders for him. His hair

was still brown as I remembered, but now it was styled perfectly, and his beard,

which he didn't have in high school, was just the right amount of scruffy. He wore a black t-shirt showcasing his toned arms, and his jeans fit him perfectly. I was also fairly certain I had caught a glimpse of a small tattoo that added to his rugged charm, but I couldn't quite make out what it was.

I stared at the flower bouquet in my hands. He remembered my favorites and asked me if I was seeing someone. Was he trying to pursue me? Surely not. I mean, after ten years we spent apart after a messy breakup, to think something like that was ridiculous. I never asked my mom about him because I didn't want to discuss what had happened, but he had likely built a life for himself here. I stalked him online occasionally, but he wasn't exactly the kind of a man to put his life out on the internet to see.

With a soft sigh, I plopped on the bed and stared at the ceiling. Sometime during the party, someone remembered to bring my suitcases to my room, which I was thankful for. Despite all the effort my mom had put into this, I didn't have the strength to go out there again.

Especially not when there was a chance I could see him again and have to engage in another conversation.

*I'm not ready for that tonight,* I thought, closing my eyes.

# Chapter 6
## Lucy

WHEN I WOKE up the next morning, I realized I had slept through the rest of the evening and the entire night. My body didn't feel *that* tired, but it seemed like I needed the rest.

When I finally forced myself to get out of bed and start my day, I put on a white sundress since Port-Cartier didn't get as much rain as Seattle. It was one of the things I missed about it —what now seemed like eternal sunshine. As I headed downstairs, I was met with the smell of coffee and pancakes. It was my favorite breakfast growing up, so of course, my mom had made it for me. It was one of her many ways to welcome me back into Port-Cartier.

"Hey, Mom," I called out as I rounded the corner to the kitchen. I stopped in my tracks,

surprised to see Ed sitting at the kitchen table. He gave me a big smile and a small wave, visibly enjoying his pancakes. "Oh, hi, Ed," I added.

"Hey, Lucy. Good to see you got proper rest."

"Sweetie," Mom said, peeking from the kitchen. She had her apron on, and her hair pulled in a messy bun on top of her head. "I made pancakes—chocolate chip ones—your favorite. I also brewed some coffee. Ed and I already had breakfast so help yourself."

My mom was an early riser, so it was no surprise that she had already eaten. My stomach grumbled in response. "Sorry, I slept through dinner last night. I guess I was more tired than I realized."

"No worries, pumpkin. I checked on you and saw that you were passed out, so I thought it would be best to let you sleep. After all, you did have a long flight."

I sat at the table with my plate piled up with pancakes, still debating on bringing up what was *truly* on my mind.

"Do you two have breakfast together every morning?" I asked, trying to understand

how close Ed and Mom were. More power to Mom if she and Ed were dating, but she

had never mentioned anything to me. And this was the kind of a thing that she'd bring up.

"I invite Ed over whenever I make pancakes," she replied suspiciously quickly. I arched my brow, and Ed patted his stomach.

"Your mom is my pancake dealer. Everyone knows she is the best cook in the county, and she keeps me well-fed."

"Tell me about it. I spent my teenage years enjoying these pancakes; it was about time I passed the torch on to someone else."

This interaction told me nothing about their relationship, if there was one, but Ed seemed nice enough. He had kind eyes, and he appeared respectful and sweet. I wanted my mom to be happy, and if her happiness was by his side, I was more than supportive.

"I'm going to have to get going soon, Lucy," my mom said, sitting at the table. "The floral shop isn't going to open itself. We'll hang out when I get back home, okay? I've stocked the fridge with groceries, so feel free to make whatever you'd like for lunch. Or you can order something. There's a cute little restaurant just around the corner..."

"Mom, I'll be fine." I gave her a small smile and chewed my pancake. She always tended to worry. Some things never changed, I guess. "Just go. I'm a big girl. I can take care of myself."

Ed looked at my mom. "I'll drive you over if you'd like, Eve."

"That would be great. Thank you," Mom responded. "I'm already late, but I wanted to ensure I was here when you woke up. Do you have any plans for today?" She gathered her things and tossed them into one of her tote bags.

"I thought I might check out downtown, hit the bookstore and coffee shop, and then we'll see where the day takes me."

"Well, have fun, and feel free to stop by the floral shop." Dashing over to me, she kissed my forehead while Ed put his mug in the sink, washing it out.

"I better take your mom to her flower shop before she loses all her marbles," he commented quietly, but it was still loud enough for her to hear.

"I heard that!" she yelled from across the hall, and I laughed.

"I'll see you around, Lucy." Ed followed my mom toward the front door.

"Love you!"

When the door slammed shut, I was left on my own. Silence surrounded me, confronting me with my encounter with Luke yesterday. It was foolish to think I wouldn't have run into him at some point, but I didn't expect it to happen so soon.

*I need to keep myself busy so I wouldn't think about it,* I decided, finishing my breakfast before heading into the town.

Port-Cartier was a small New England town in that swelled in the summer due to tourists. It wasn't as popular as the bigger town next to it, but that was the way the residents preferred it. The downtown ran parallel to the beach. Each side of the street had different businesses, with the restaurant and coffee shop sitting just feet from the beach. My home was a short walk to downtown, and since I didn't have a car, my choice was made for me. Growing up, I had always walked everywhere—until I started dating Luke in our sophomore year, who insisted on driving me everywhere.

I had forgotten how much it had sucked to walk in the summer with the humidity. By the time I reached The Book Nook, my hair was sticking to my face and neck and starting to grow a little frizzy. For that reason, in Seattle, with the rain and dampness, I had often

kept my hair piled on top of my head. I rarely showed my natural curls anymore, but maybe that was another change that needed to be implemented.

I stepped inside the bookstore, breathing a sigh of relief as the air conditioning hit me. The Book Nook was in a red brick building with large windows that let in plenty of natural light. Even from outside, I got a good peek at the neatly lined shelves with a wide selection of books of all different genres.

"Lucy!" a tall, black man at the front counter called out, sliding his glasses from the top of his head to his nose to inspect me further.

"Gabe, is that you?" I stepped forward hesitantly. "Oh my God, how are you?"

Gabe came out from behind the counter to hug me. We had been friends in high school—not the super close kind, but it was still the kind of friendship that was comfortable.

"Fabulous as usual! I heard you were coming back, but I didn't believe it until I saw it with my own eyes."

I smiled. "I didn't realize that you had moved back to Port-Cartier."

"Yeah, well, that's what happens when you drop off the face of the earth."

I cringed as a pang of guilt spread through me. When I left, I left everything and everyone behind—aside from my mom. I cut all the contact with everyone I once knew, thinking it was exactly what I needed for a fresh start. Back then, I didn't realize how that choice affected those around me. "I'm sorry; I just needed to get away from here after everything that happened. I wasn't thinking straight."

"Pssh, it's water under the bridge. My husband and I moved back a few years ago and

bought the bookstore from Maggie, who was just about to retire. It's always been Marcus' dream to own a bookstore, so we made it happen."

"Marcus? The one you used to bicker with constantly?"

Another smile spread across his face. "That's right."

"Well, I'd love to see him sometime."

"We'll arrange something. He's out getting some inventory, but we can schedule a dinner together." The phone rang, pulling Gabe away from our conversation. "I've got to go but look around and let me know if you need anything."

I moved through the stacks, pulling out books to read the blurbs. If there was one way to get my mind off things—it was this. Reading was something I had always enjoyed, ever since I was a kid. And I'd need at least a few books to tide me over while I was here on vacation. The selection I left the bookstore with ranged from a thriller, over to a mystery novel, all the way to non-fiction. I stayed away from romance. I was not in the right mindset to read about couples who got their happily ever after.

Despite having a cup of coffee with my breakfast, I was

craving another cup by noon. Sailor had said I was an addict. I'd retorted that I liked the finer things in life. And coffee was one of them.

I headed next door to Brew Haha, Port-Cartier's famous coffee shop. The owner bought it during my senior year of high school, and it quickly became a popular hangout for young and old alike. As I entered, nearly all the tables were full, especially those on the ocean-front patio. The décor had changed somewhat since I last had been here, but they kept the bohemian vibe.

I got in line and browsed the menu, trying to figure out if I wanted to go with my old

faithful drink or try something new. A silky voice appeared behind me, sending a shudder down my spine. "Do you remember what you used to get?"

I whirled around, facing face to face with a broad, muscular chest belonging to Luke.

"I was actually just checking out the menu." I was determined not to be flustered by him again. Last night was bad enough.

*I walked into Brew Haha, hand in hand with Luke. This was becoming our new after-school routine, one I hoped to keep for many years.*

*"You two are adorable. You'll be married before you know it," the owner behind the*

*counter told us. I looked up at Luke, unable to hold back the smile that tugged at my lips. We had it all planned out. We would go to college together, and then we'd get married and return to Port-Cartier, where Luke would take over his family's shipbuilding business. I was going to the community college near Luke since he was going to an engineering college. Luke was getting a marine engineering and architecture degree, which would pay off in the long run. The local community college didn't have the floral artistry degree I wanted, but I would get a business degree and then figure out the rest from there. I just wanted to be with Luke. Things would be hard for a little while, but it would all work out in the end.*

*"You bet. I have every intention of marrying this girl soon…"*

"Next!" the guy at the front called out, and I was still staring at Luke.

"That's you, sweetheart," he pointed out. The words made me weak in my knees, and I quickly shook my head to pull myself out of this trance.

*Jesus, I need to get a grip on myself around him.*

I swiftly turned around and directed my attention to the barista. "I'll have an iced French vanilla cold brew to go, please," I told him.

"And I'll have my usual. You can put it both on my tab, Riley."

"Will do," the barista said with a grin, turning to get our order ready.

I hated the idea of silence around him, so I quickly said, "You don't have to do that. I can pay for my coffee."

Luke moved beside me, looking down at me. "Consider it a welcome home gift."

I bit my bottom lip and then let out a small sigh. "Fine, but I'll get the next one."

"Done." Luke grinned. I realized what I had just said was too late. That meant there *would* be a next time. I had walked right into that one, and there was no backing out now. I narrowed my eyes at him. The move made Luke break out into a full-on smile.

"What are you doing here? Are you stalking me?"

"I come here for coffee every day. If anything, you'd be considered a stalker."

I rolled my eyes at his words. "I just wanted a cup of coffee, Luke. Don't flatter yourself."

"And you're getting it now," he retorted.

The barista handed us our drinks.

"Thank you for the coffee," I mumbled as I grabbed my

coffee and marched out of the coffee shop, eager to put distance between Luke and me. It was too easy to fall back into our old habits, but I couldn't forget there were ten years and *a lot* of hurt between us. The end of my relationship with Jason was bad enough; I couldn't deal with this, too.

Luke followed me out. "Luce, wait up!"

"What now—" I stopped, turning around…and running right into Luke. "Fuck!" My iced coffee splattered down my front, instantly turning my white sundress tan. Luke didn't fair too well, either. His pants took the brunt of the spill. Thank God all I had was an iced drink and that Luke had managed not to crush his coffee between the two of us.

"Shit, I'm sorry, Luce, I didn't know you were going to turn around that quickly. Here, my house is just around the corner. I have some clothes you can change into."

"I am *not* going to your house, Luke," I told him firmly, ignoring the people who passed by. Luke's brows furrowed.

"I'm just trying to help. This was an accident. But if you'd prefer to walk around with a giant coffee stain…"

I sighed. "Lead the way," I said, gesturing before me.

My sandals squeaked as I followed Luke. At least this way, I got to admire the way his jeans clung to his ass. You could bounce a quarter off that ass. Luke had always been fit but now he was not only fit but muscular too. He filled out his t-shirt and jeans. I tried not to drool at the sight in front of me.

As if he could sense my thoughts, he turned around, slowing down a few paces and restricting my dirty vision.

We only had to travel a few houses down. He turned onto a cobblestone walkway leading up to a small house with a porch with a swinging bench. The house was painted sage green and had a small garden around it. I could tell Luke tried his best to keep it going. God bless him, but he was never the one with a green thumb in our relationship.

My steps faltered. Luke turned.

"You...you bought the house?" I asked, my voice just a whisper. Luke rubbed his neck. It was his tell for when he was nervous.

"Yeah, I bought it a few years ago, and I've been slowly fixing it ever since."

"You've done a great job." My eyes threatened to fill with tears, but I quickly blinked them away. This was the house we had picked out our senior year of high school. It had been on the market for years. It needed a lot of work, but we would buy it together.

"Come on," Luke said, and we walked up the front steps to the porch. He held open the front door as I stepped inside.

I was immediately pulled in by the scent of him. It was a pine and musk scent that

put me at ease. The home was sparsely decorated, but everything had been updated. The floors were made of solid hardwood. The living room bled into the kitchen, which had been updated with new cabinetry and appliances.

"It's beautiful in here, Luke."

Luke put his hands in his pockets. "I still have more to do, but it's coming along. Anyway, I'll go get you some clothes."

# Chapter 7
## Lucy

AS LUKE LEFT, my gaze swept over the place, settling on the photos that hung above the

fireplace mantle. Familiar faces stared at me from moments captured to last for an eternity, smiling. Luke had two brothers—Landon and Logan. It was always an ongoing joke that their parents had a thing for names that started with L, but I thought it was sweet.

Landon was the oldest; then there was Luke, and then Logan. They were all about two years apart. There were also photos of his parents, who were, funnily enough, named Linda and Levi. Luke was a spitting image of his father; it was like staring into the future and getting an opportunity to see what he would look like in a few decades.

I had so much love for all of them. When we dated, they were practically a second family to me and welcomed me into their home with open arms. His parents, as well as my own mom, were our biggest cheerleaders. When we broke up, we didn't only break our own hearts—we broke theirs, too.

I took another step to the left, finding a photograph of us that instantly drew a smile to my face. It was a candid photo from our senior prom. The dress I wore that night was a crime against humanity, but it faded compared to the adoring look that locked between us.

*Luke stepped closer to me, placing one of his hands on my waist while the other held mine. Our fingers interlocked, and I couldn't help but stop smiling.*

*"You know, a lot of people are skeptical about high school relationships, but I know this is it for us," he told me softly as we swayed to the soft hum of the music around us. I rolled my eyes playfully.*

*"Luke, you know we're dating, right? You don't need to sweet-talk me like this anymore if you want to make out. I'll gladly do it anyway."*

*A cheeky grin crossed his lips. "Duly noted, but I'm not trying to sweet talk you into anything. Someday, we'll be dancing like this at our wedding."*

Behind me, Luke cleared his throat. I whirled around. My cheeks flushed like I had been caught doing something highly illegal.

"Here's some clothes for you. It's all I have, but it should fit you," he said, handing over sweatpants and a black t-shirt. I grabbed the clothes from him, and our hands touched for a fraction of a second, but that was enough to make me shiver. "The bathroom is just there. There's a shower in there too. I put a towel in there if you would like to take one. Unfortunately, I only have three-in-one shower gel…"

"Luke," I groaned. Some things never changed, apparently. No matter how much I tried to convince him that products like that sacrificed quality in at least one of their supposed functions, he swore by them back then. And now.

"Don't judge me until you try it." He put his hands up. "If you toss your clothes out, I can put them in a bag for you."

"Thank you," I said softly before heading into the bathroom, desperate to put some space between us. The photographs certainly had memories flood my mind. Why did he still have that photograph of us hanging on the wall?

Did that mean he wasn't seeing anyone? I couldn't imagine any woman being okay with a photo of his ex-girlfriend in his living room.

Locking the door behind me, I looked around the bathroom. It was simple yet elegant—like the rest of his home. I caught a glimpse of myself in the mirror, staring at my reflection.

"You need to get a hold of yourself," I whispered. This was precisely what I wanted to avoid. I was supposed to be this sophisticated woman who left her past behind her and was now living in a big city and had a great job...but also had a shitty boyfriend and no place to live, apparently.

I couldn't delve deeper into everything wrong with my life now. Instead, I stripped off my clothes and tossed them outside the door before starting the shower. I pulled my hair into a messy bun on top of my head but suspected the moisture would do its thing and make the curls even more prominent. And I knew Luke would like that. My curls were always one of his favorite things about me.

The warm water relaxed my tense muscles, but it did very little to clear my mind. I should have seen this coming, coming here and poking at my past like that. I took my time, not quite ready to face him yet.

Once I was confident I pulled myself together, I slipped into the clothes he gave me. Instantly, his scent hit me. How was it possible that he smelled so similarly to how he did all those years ago? And, more importantly, why did his scent remain so embedded in my mind for a decade?

The shirt he had given me was one of his beloved oversized shirts that I always used to try to steal away from him when we were younger. I was surprised that he still had it, considering he had grown well into his muscular frame. Wearing this shirt was likely the closest I'd ever come to having him embrace me again.

# Chapter 8
## Luke

WHEN LUCY EXITED THE BATHROOM, I sat on the couch and waited for her. My clothes were certainly not her style anymore, but I couldn't deny she looked beautiful. I stood up, approaching her to inspect her further while keeping a respectful distance between us.

"I can't believe you still have this shirt," she said, tugging at the black fabric. Her hair was pulled into a messy bun on her head, which I had always loved. "There is *no* way you can still fit in this."

"You're right," I admitted, taking another step toward her. She stalled in her spot, observing me. "It doesn't fit me anymore. I kept it because it reminded me of you."

It was an honest admission of my feelings. For as long as I could remember, I envisioned her back in my life, wearing that exact shirt. It felt like somewhat of a dream to have that happen again. If it was, indeed, a dream, I didn't want to ever wake up. I wanted to stay trapped here for an eternity and never leave her side.

"Luke…" She trailed off. The words fell from my lips before I could fully think through what I would say.

"I'm sorry. I can't possibly tell you how sorry I am for all the hurt I've caused you. A day doesn't go by that I don't hate myself for it," I told her, reaching for her cheek. My thumb trailed over her flawless skin. She was so soft, so warm, and every inch of me itched to be closer to her. "I have thought about you every single day for the past ten years. You haven't left my mind for a damn minute, sweetheart. I need you to know that."

The yearning that had accumulated over the past decade guided my body, and I had very little say in what I did. One moment, I towered over her, and my head dipped lower the next. My lips found hers, and I kissed her tenderly, hoping to tell her everything that had remained unspoken for the past decade. I expected her to push me away, but she didn't.

And that only made me greedier.

My arms bracketed her slender body, my hands on her hips as I pulled her closer. The most primal need to have her awoke inside me, and I had a sneaking suspicion that it had no intention of ever leaving. A small moan escaped her lips, coming out muffled against my lips and carrying away any last shreds of self-control that I once had. I was a starved man, and she was everything I ever wanted.

We stumbled backwards until her back bumped against the wall behind her, our kiss growing more heated with each second. I found the hem of her sweatpants, about to pull them down when she finally broke free from the spell of our kiss and tilted her head to the side.

"Luke, stop," she said, and she didn't need to tell me twice. Instantly, I stepped back, giving her some space as the realization of what had happened sunk into my mind. I cursed at myself and the fact that I allowed my lust to overcome my true intentions.

The last thing I wanted was for her to think I was trying to get into her pants. I wanted to make this work. I wanted us to have a proper shot. And now, I was faced with the possibility that I may have messed it all up.

"I'm sorry, I just—"

"It's fine." Lucy held her hand up to stop me from talking. She took a moment to draw in a deep breath before she finally dared to look me right in the eyes. "Thank you for everything, but I think I should go. I'll give you your clothes back once I wash them."

"Give me a second, and I'll put your clothes into—"

"Don't worry about it. I'll come pick them up when I drop yours off," she spoke over me. There was suddenly this need in her to put as much distance between us as possible, and I didn't like it the slightest bit.

Were we at the point of no return?

"Luce, please, give me a moment," I pleaded, wanting to make things right. And she gave me the moment I asked for, even if I didn't deserve it. "I got carried away. I wasn't planning on something like that happening—I just…I missed you. I meant what I said."

She pressed her lips into a thin line, silent for a second. "It wasn't just you. I participated, too. But it doesn't mean we should be doing it," Lucy said. "We can't do this, Luke."

My chest tightened at her words, but I wouldn't push her. I still hoped that things would work between us, but I wouldn't force her into anything she didn't feel comfortable doing. If what she needed right now was space—then that was what I would give to her.

"Let me drive you home, at least," I offered, even if it meant driving silently. I didn't care. I wanted to make it up to her somehow. But much like I expected, she turned that offer down quickly.

"I appreciate it, but I'd rather walk. I need to clear my head." Lucy was now at the door. I knew she wasn't leaving forever—not yet, at least—but the sight still tugged at my heart.

"Okay. Get home safe," was all I said as I watched her leave. As silence surrounded me again, I realized there was no going back. Even if just briefly, I experienced what life with her by my side would be again, and I wasn't sure I could let it go. Not without a fight.

I messed up once; I wasn't going to do it again.

# Chapter 9
## Lucy

AS I STEPPED inside the house, I was thankful to find it empty. The last thing I wanted to do was face my mom in Luke's clothes. Especially with the chaos that resided in my mind. It would bring so many unwanted questions, and I wasn't sure I'd be able to answer them just yet.

The moment I was in my room, I changed out of his clothes and put on some shorts and a t-shirt. Right away, the lack of his scent cleared my head slightly, but I found my heart aching to be surrounded by it again.

*Don't be ridiculous,* I told myself again. I was acting like I was in high school all over again, and to say it was unacceptable was an understatement. Before I could feel sorry for myself even more, I dashed into the kitchen to whip up a sandwich. It wasn't until my stomach rumbled in protest that I realized how hungry I was. With a sandwich in one hand and a glass of orange juice in the other, I headed out to the back porch to soak in the sun.

The view from here was stunning, with the ocean twinkling softly in the distance beneath the swirls of the clouds. It was one of the reasons that had my mom sold on this house. Now that I was older, I could fully appreciate why.

The longer I sat there, engulfed in silence, the more unwanted thoughts weaseled back into my mind.

I had been here one day and had already tried to jump Luke's bones, and it couldn't happen again—under any circumstances. I planned for my trip to last for fourteen days, so it meant I only had thirteen left.

Thirteen days left to avoid him in this incredibly small town. It was a totally plausible idea, wasn't it? The only issue with my plan was that I had to return his clothes at some point and retrieve mine that I had left behind.

My phone buzzed in my pocket, and I retrieved it to find a message from the only person I could count on to cheer me up right now.

> SAILOR: How's everything going? I expected more updates, girl!

> ME: Everything's fine. I'm just enjoying the sunshine; I haven't been online much.

> SAILOR: You don't say! Send a pic or two!

> SAILOR: Also, have you seen him?

I hesitated for a moment. Sailor knew every part of me— including the one I tried to keep buried deep down for as long as I could remember. It was natural that she'd ask this. The urge to lie was there for whatever reason. I didn't want to admit it to myself, let alone to someone else.

> ME: I have, but nothing is going on. I'm not dating again. Remember my last relationship?

SAILOR: Fair enough. Still, you should probably get laid, if even causally.

SAILOR: The best way to get over someone is to get under someone ;)

ME: The only thing I want to be under right now is the sun.

I didn't realize how long I had been outside until I heard the front door open. My mom was back, apparently. I headed back inside, greeting her with a small smile as she carried bags with groceries inside. I grabbed one, helping her put the items she brought into the cupboards. One thing that I could count on never changing was the order in my mom's kitchen. It remained the same, even a decade ago, so I knew exactly where to put whatever I reached for.

"How was your day?" I asked her.

"Good, I was able to book another wedding for this winter. This is going to be a good year for business." Pride spread through me—aside from me, her business was my mom's pride and joy. I was glad it was going well.

"That's amazing, Mom. I'm so proud of you."

A smile reflected on her face. "Thanks, pumpkin. Another great thing happened today, too."

"Oh yeah, what's that?" I leaned against the kitchen island.

"I signed you up to work the food tent at Hometown Days this weekend." My expression fell, and my eyebrows furrowed together. I didn't...expect that.

"Well, I thought I was just going to visit. I wasn't planning on participating, Mom..." I stammered. With everything going on, the last thing I wanted to do was be surrounded by people for days. I came here to find peace and clear my mind, but my mom was impossible to say no to.

"I know, but the historical society needed more volunteers, and I can't help since I'll be

helping to judge the pie-baking contest. Plus, you don't have to work the entire time. I signed you up for a two-hour shift at the beginning of the fair." As she looked at me with her hope-filled eyes, it was impossible to say no.

I sighed, opening the fridge to put the eggs she bought there. "Fine, but I'm only doing this because I love you."

Excitement flooded her face and she clapped her hands together. "Perfect! You won't regret it, you'll see," she said. "By the way, I heard you ran into Luke at the coffee shop today."

I laid my head against the fridge door. *Of course*, she already knew. "I forgot how quickly news travels around town."

My mom came to my side and hugged me. "Unfortunately, this town runs on gossip…or rather, fortunately, in my case."

"Mom!" I laughed, shaking my head as she tightened her grip around me.

"What? An old lady has to get her jollies somewhere!"

More laughter rumbled from my chest to the point where I could barely breathe. "One, you're not old, and two, you're ridiculous." As my laugh subdued, a pang of guilt quickly replaced it. How many moments like these did I miss out on because I was so eager to escape the moment Luke and I broke up?

"So, what's the story there?"

"There's no story. I know you're hoping for something… spectacular, but there's nothing like that." I felt bad that I was lying to her, but telling her the truth was not an option. She'd get her hopes up and try to push me to pursue a relationship with him again. Her intentions were good, but it wasn't what

I needed now, just like it wasn't what I needed a decade ago. "I ran into him at the coffee shop. I spilt my coffee all over him and myself. He

gave me some clothes to wear home. That's it."

"I see. So, why are you blushing, then?" She cocked her eyebrow at me. Apparently, nothing got past her.

"Because of the weather, Mom. I'm not used to heat like this back in Seattle. Sorry to disappoint your gossip-loving heart." I rubbed her arm. "Now, why don't we order pizza for

dinner? I'm starving." I hoped my mom would take the bait and change the subject. Luke was the last thing I wanted to talk about tonight. My mom pressed her lips together before she gave me a small nod.

"Nice try to avoid the topic," she said with a sigh. "Sure, we can get pizza for dinner."

# Chapter 10
## Lucy

OVER THE NEXT FEW DAYS, I managed to avoid Luke, mainly because I didn't leave my home. I still counted it a success, but a girl could only stay locked up for so long.

By the time the weekend arrived, I was going stir-crazy, and I actually found myself thankful that today was the start of Hometown Days. It was finally an excuse to leave the house.

My mom put me in charge of working at the food tent, so hopefully, I could hide in the back and get my shift done— away from people and, more importantly, away from Luke.

Hometown Days was Port-Cartier's annual summer festival. It was their kick-off to the

summer tourist season. There were food vendors, baking contests, exhibitions and many craft vendors. It lured the tourists in like no other event and for a good reason. It was spectacular, and everyone put so much effort into their part. And though I wasn't here by choice, I planned to do the same.

I took in the smell of the fried food as I walked by the various food tents, looking for the Polish sausage tent my mom had signed me up for. Most of the Hometown Days tents extended down the coast, so the tourists could enjoy fantastic food and the stunning view of the sea in front of them.

I found the tent wedged between the dough boy truck and the French fry stall. I hesitated for a moment before I approached the old woman at the front of the tent, giving her a small smile.

"Hi, I'm Lucy, and I'm here for my volunteer shift."

The woman looked me up and down with a frown before she said, "You're late."

I grimaced. I didn't want to start on the wrong foot, or it would be a long two hours. I also didn't want to let down my mom. She counted on me to do this.

"Sorry, I couldn't find the tent. I'm happy to stay longer if you would like."

The woman said nothing but motioned for me to follow her. "You can cut the onions and green peppers for the sandwiches. Cut them into long slices, and then Johanna will cook them with sausages for the sandwiches." The woman gestured to several overflowing baskets of green peppers and onions. My eyes practically bugged out of my head.

"You need all of these cut?" I asked. That seemed like a lot of work for a two-hour shift.

"Whatever you don't cut will be the next person's job. We're the most popular tent, and we get *a lot* of business." The woman puffed out her chest in pride.

"Okay, then, I guess I will just get started." The woman, who I still didn't know the name of, passed me an apron, and I put it on before I got to work.

I started cutting an assortment of onions and green peppers, and it wasn't long before the onions had tears rolling down my face. I wiped them away using the bottom of my apron, but that only made my eyes worse.

"God, I hate onions!" I grumbled. Behind me, Johanna chuckled.

"Tell me about it. That's why we have the newer volunteers do it," she commented, and I found myself envious of the clarity of her vision. Especially as my eyes continued to tear up, causing me to lose sight of what I was doing.

I saw it before I felt it happen—the sharp pain that was quickly followed by red liquid soaking my pale skin. I tried to blink the tears away to assess the damage and keep my fingers away from the food.

"Shit!" I swore, and both Johanna and Grouchy Pants approached me.

"What happened?" the older woman asked. It would've been helpful to know her name at this point.

"I cut my finger. I'll be fin—"

"You need to get that looked at," Johanna interrupted, "We can't have you bleeding all over the food."

"I can put a glove on and have it looked at later," I retorted, though the sting quickly spread through my hand. "I want to finish cutting these."

"No one will want to see blood, even in a glove." The older woman's tone was a little softer as I clutched my wounded finger.

"How bad is it?" I asked them, and she gave me what I could only describe as a smile for the first time since I came here. Johanna inspected it closer.

"It's not too bad. The med tent is just over there. Have it looked at and bandaged, and then you can come back and finish your shift. The food tents open in twenty minutes. That will be plenty of time for you to come back. Plus, Margaret, can cut while you are gone."

Margaret, formerly known as Grouchy Pants, grunted and turned away, so I assumed she wanted me to get this done as quickly as possible. That was one thing we agreed on.

I didn't bother to take my apron off as I made my way to the med-tent. My finger hurt and looked worse than it was, but I was sure I'd forget all about it once it was bandaged. At least the onions were no longer assaulting my eyes.

I entered the tent, which was set up like a makeshift hospital, with a few reclining-type chairs on the left side and supplies on the right wall. Many tourists weren't used to the heat, which was the main reason the tent was there.

"Hey, Luce," a familiar voice called out. I turned to my left to see Luke sitting on a stool. Fuck, I guess my tactics to avoid him had failed me today. "What brings you here?" he asked, concern showing across his face as his eyes drifted lower.

"I was cutting food, and my knife slipped. I ended up cutting my finger. The better question is, what are you doing here?" I asked him in return as I approached his spot. I may as well have him get it done now. If I were to avoid him, it would only make things more awkward. "Do you have medical experience?"

"I did some EMT work in college," he explained as he retrieved his supplies, still looking worried. "I'll get you bandaged up. Wait, are you crying?"

"No, the onions are potent suckers." I tried wiping my eyes with my apron, but that made it much worse. It was too late by the time I realized the apron likely had onion juice on it, and I smeared it all over my eyes. "They feel like they are on fire right now."

"Here, let's rinse your eyes. We have an eye wash station over here. Come on." Luke

held out his hand to help me up. I took his hand, his warmth seeping into me. He led me

over to the station, guiding my every movement. "Put your head over the sink, and I will pour some of the sterilized water over your eyes." I leaned my head over the sink and Luke carefully poured water over my eyes. The relief was immediate. I let out a groan.

"God, that feels amazing." I sighed. "Thank you. You're a lifesaver."

Luke cleared his throat. "That should do it. Hang tight, and I'll get you a towel to wipe your face with before we take care of your finger." I stood up with my eyes closed until Luke handed me a towel. I put out my hand and felt a hard wall of muscle instead.

"Oh, sorry," I said, my cheeks heating up. Instead of guiding me toward the towel, Luke gently patted it against my face. As I finally opened my eyes, I found Luke looking down at me. The height difference seemed even more prominent after the decade we spent away from each other. He stood just over 6' while I was at a meagre 5'2" on a good day.

"Let's take a peek at your finger now."

# Chapter 11
## Luke

A FINGER CUT wasn't the end of the world, but for some reason, it felt that way when it came to Lucy. The urge to protect her had been planted in me from the first time we saw each other, and today was no exception. We made our way back to my spot, and she settled in the reclining chair.

"Are you still as squeamish as you were about blood?"

"Nah." She waved her good hand. "When you have eighteen second graders losing teeth or scraping their knees over nine months, you tend to lose your squeamishness."

"Second graders, huh? That's what you do?" I knew it was what she did, but I tried to keep her distracted as I disinfected her wound. It didn't look too good, but I hoped once I cleared the blood, I'd be able to properly see the damage.

Her mom shared details about her life here and there, but hearing it from her would've been nice.

"Yeah. That's what I do. It wasn't my original plan, but—"

"Luke Puke," Logan called out as he strode into the tent, and I fought the urge to groan. I *hated* that nickname more than anything. I puked in my bed one time, and I never heard the end of it. "Mom sent me to come help you in the med-tent."

Lucy laughed at the nickname, which instantly drew Logan's attention. He quickly approached us, standing at a similar height to me. Where I was all dark features and hair, Logan took on the lighter features of the family. He had a bent nose from his football days, a strong jaw, and light facial hair that matched his hair.

"Lucy Goosey!" he said in surprise as he dove at her, nearly tackling the entire chair backward. Logan had a thing about nicknames. It was like he was unable to call anyone by their actual name. And Lucy, for once, didn't seem to mind it.

"Easy," I warned him, and only then did he retreat a step back. "She already has a cut finger; she doesn't need a concussion, too." The shift in Lucy's posture was nearly instant. The moment Logan was around us, she seemed more relaxed, ignoring my warning as she reached for him.

"Aw, I missed you too, Logan. It's good to see you."

My brother looked at me briefly, giving me a slight smirk. "Did you hear that, big brother? Lucy Goosey missed me. Maybe that means I finally have a chance!" I glowered at him.

"I'm sorry to disappoint you, but no one has a chance with me. I just broke up with a guy, and I'm leaving in ten days to return to Seattle." I straightened at her words. The last thing that was currently on my mind was her finger, which I was nearly done patching up.

There was another thing that struck me. Realistically, I knew staying here was likely not her long-term plan, but only ten days wasn't enough to win her over again. I needed more time.

Logan continued with his nonsense. "So, maybe a fling then? I'm up for anything!"

"You're ridiculous." Lucy couldn't keep the smile from her face, which…bothered me. It shouldn't have, but it did. I ached to be the reason behind smiles like that again.

"Get out of here," I grumbled at Logan, pushing him out of the tent flap. I wanted privacy with Lucy again, especially if she was planning to leave so soon. Logan waved at both of us

"Alright, fine, Luke Puke. I'll tell Mom you didn't need any help. And bye, Lucy Goosey! Call me if you want to fool around." Logan winked at her.

"Oh, now you're asking for it." I got out of my seat and rushed after him. I know Logan didn't mean anything by it—he knew how much Lucy and I were in love back when we dated, just as he likely knew how much she still meant to me, but it didn't mean he didn't deserve to be roughed up a little bit.

I tackled him to the ground outside, and we wrestled around for a good few seconds. Neither of us could stop smiling before he finally managed to break free from my grasp and speed off to Mom. Lucy came out of the tent, her lips tugged upward.

"Roughhousing again, huh? It's gotten you two into trouble more times than I can count," she commented. I shrugged.

"Some things never change."

"And some do, apparently. Logan got one on you, hm?" Lucy asked, gesturing to the grass stain on my white shirt.

"He's a lot bigger now, but I can still take him," I assured her. "Anyway, your finger is all good now, but if you..." I trailed off. I wanted to tell her to find me if she needed anything. I desperately wanted to keep her presence around me, but I also didn't want to push her. "I'll be here if you cut yourself again."

"Wow," she chuckled, "you're *that* confident of my cutting skills?"

"You have many talents, Luce, but cutting vegetables isn't one of them."

She didn't say another word. Instead, she rolled her eyes playfully and strolled back to her tent.

# Chapter 12

LUKE PATCHING my finger made the rest of my shift easier to bear, especially after seeing Logan. After ten years away from this place, I *almost* forgot how much I missed the Everett family.

My shift passed in a flurry of sausages—and not the fun kind.

"Okay, kid," Margaret told me as she walked to the back of the tent. "Your replacement is here." I was happy to be done cutting onions and green peppers. I'd be fine if I never saw another sausage sandwich.

*"Oh, come on. I really don't feel like going," I grumbled, still wrapped in the sheets. It was far too early to get up, let alone to go to the Hometown Days festival. It happened every year. And while it was appealing to tourists, I had seen it far too many times to consider it interesting.*

*"Are you saying you're not up for a date?" Luke questioned me. He was settled in behind me on the bed, with his arm wrapped around my body. Ever since he first slept over without my mom knowing, he made it a habit to come here now and then. Nothing happened—and it wouldn't until I was ready for it, but I couldn't deny that waking up next to him was nice.*

*"I am up for a date. I just don't see why we need to go to the festival..."*

*"Well, you'll never know unless you come and join me." He showered the back of my shoulder with tender kisses, and I already knew I stood no chance. I would've done anything he asked me to do.*

*And I was right. We moved through the endless tents of vendors who all came to display their best products. They had even set up a mini arcade this year. I eyed all the plush animals that had been displayed, setting my eyes on a soft, brown teddy bear.*

*"You know, I feel like I deserve one of these for coming with you today," I told him, gesturing toward the teddy bear I wanted. "I think I want that one."*

*A smile reached his eyes, and I knew at that moment he would have done anything to win it for me.*

"Lucy?" The voice pulled me back into reality, and I found Margaret standing before me with her hands on her hips.

"Sorry, I got lost in thought. What were you saying?"

"I said your shift is done. You're free to go."

My brows furrowed together. To my surprise, my shift ended much sooner than I expected. Despite the initial reluctance and the minor mishap of cutting my finger, I found myself contemplating the idea of doing it again.

After saying goodbye to Margaret and Johanna, I wandered by the other vendors for a little longer before returning home. I didn't run into Luke again, which was probably for the best. I could only handle seeing him *once* today. As I strolled down the street toward my home, I grabbed my phone and called Sailor, who I *knew* was still awaiting updates.

The video call only rang once before she picked up with a big smile.

"Girl! Oh, my God! I was wondering when you'd finally call me," she chirped. Sailor was on her balcony, desperate for the sun that the grey sky above Seattle didn't allow yet. "How's everything going?"

"Good, everything is good," I told her, lifting my bandaged finger into the frame. "Though I did cut my finger today." Her expression quickly fell.

"What? How? You've got to be more careful."

"I was volunteering at the Hometown Days festival." I then quickly added before she could question it further, "My mom signed me up. Don't ask."

"How's your mom, by the way?"

"She's great. I think she may have a boyfriend, but I'm not entirely sure. She hasn't talked about it, but I figure she will when she's ready." I knew what it was like to have everyone know your business, so I would let her tell me in her own time.

Sailor gasped loudly. "No. Way. Tell me everything about him!"

"Well, his name is Ed, and he's a police officer. He's sweet, and I think he makes her happy, so I'm happy for her," I told her. "How's everything back in Seattle?"

"It's good. By the way, Jason tried to contact me. Ugh. That asshole."

*Jason.* With my sudden return to the past, I entirely forgot about the reason why I was here in the first place. The breakup still stung, but this town did its magic and had me thinking about it much less.

I waved my hand at her. "Just ignore him. He's not worth your time."

"I want to ignore him, but it's hard when all I can think about is setting him on fire." Sailor smiled sweetly. I chuckled, even if her words drew attention from one of the neighbors. I could only pray they knew she was joking.

When I stood in front of my house, I gave Sailor another small smile. "Look, I've got to go now. Thank you for keeping me company...if you're free, I could call you later. And you can also talk to your favorite person in the world." I paused. "My mom."

Sailor laughed. "You bet! I'm in. Love you, girl!"

"Love you, too." I hung up and headed into the house. I heard my mom rummaging through something in the living room when I opened the door.

"Mom?" I called out.

"Right here!" she yelled out. As I moved into the living room, I found her on the ladder she brought in from the garage, rummaging through one of the wall cupboards.

"Mom, what are you..." I trailed off as catastrophe unraveled before my own two eyes. The next few seconds played out in slow motion. In a fragment of a moment, my mom slipped and fell from the ladder, landing on the wooden floor with a loud thud. I heard the crack of her bones, which was quickly followed by a flood of pained curse words.

"Mom!" I yelled out the moment everything settled in, rushing toward her. She was still on the floor, and her right foot was in an unnatural position that sent a shudder down my spine. She definitely broke something. As I crouched beside her, I didn't dare to try to move her as panic whirled inside my mind.

"I'm...okay, pumpkin. Oh, God!"

My hands were shaking as I dialed 911, barely able to focus on anything the dispatcher was saying. I needed to get my mom to the hospital.

# Chapter 13
# Luke

AS MY PHONE BUZZED, I was surprised to see Ed's number on it. It wasn't often that he called me—if there was anyone to call from my family, it was my older brother, Landon, who worked as a doctor at the hospital in the nearby city of Rockwood. Still, I picked up without a moment of hesitation, worried that something had happened.

"Ed? Is everything all right?"

"Not really, Luke. I'm calling because Eve was hurt." My heart dropped in my chest.

"Hurt? How? Is she—"

"She fell from the ladder in her living room. I told her a million times to wait for me when she needs to get things like that done, but you know what she's like." He sighed.

"Is she going to be okay?" I quickly asked, and then a nagging question popped into my mind. "Is Lucy okay?"

"That's why I'm calling. Lucy's pretty shaken up. I was there when Eve was taken in the ambulance, and she couldn't stop crying. I'm pretty sure she's still crying in the hospital, so she could use a shoulder to cry on. I don't want her to be alone."

"I got it," I said, grabbing my jacket already. Thankfully, I was done with my shift at the medical tent. "They're in Rock-wood, right?"

"Yeah. I already called Landon, too. To keep an eye on her and all. I'm still not done with my shift, but I'll be there when I finish work."

"Don't worry about it." I rushed toward my car. "I'll keep an eye on both of them."

It took me thirty-five minutes to get to the Rockwood General Hospital. On my way there, I called Landon, who, for once, didn't return my call. I hoped it meant he was in with Lucy's mom. As I ran into the waiting room, I found her seated at one of the plastic chairs, with her arms wrapped around her as she sobbed inconsolably. Her eyes were red from crying, and her nose from blowing it. The sight was enough to shatter my heart.

"Lucy..." I called out as I walked over to her. The moment I was beside her, my arms wrapped around her, pulling her into a tight embrace. And she let me. She sobbed into my chest, unable to string together a sentence, and I gave her all the time she needed. "She's going to be okay, Luce," I promised. I knew Landon would do everything he could to ensure she got the best care possible. "And you will be fine, too. I'll stay with you."

"Thank you," she whispered, sniffling. "But you don't have to. I'm sure you have a million things you need to do..." Despite her words, she was still gripping me tightly and not letting go. Nothing I needed to do could compare to this—being by her side when she needed me. I missed out on a chance to do it for a decade, and I wasn't about to let it happen now.

"Why don't I go find Landon to see what's happening with your mom?"

She looked up at me with a slight nod.

My hand clasped around hers. "Come with me," I told her, not wanting to leave her alone for a second. For as long as I could remember, it had always been just her and her mom, so it wasn't surprising that this left her completely shaken up.

Lucy was silent as we strolled toward my brother's office. Just when I was about to knock, the door opened, and I nearly bumped into him. While I had the darker traits in the family and Logan lighter, Landon was in the perfect middle, with warm, brown hair and brown eyes to match. He was a few inches taller than me, too.

"I was just about to come find you," he said. Lucy started sobbing again, but I knew my brother's expression. The news he was about to deliver wasn't bad.

"How is she?" Lucy barely managed to force the words out between the sobs.

"Lucy," my brother said, placing his hand on her shoulder. "She's okay. She's in surgery right now. The fall was pretty bad, and she broke her bones in multiple areas. The recovery before her will be lengthy, but she's in stable condition. We suspect she may have a concussion, too, but that's about it. After her surgery, she'll need to stay in the hospital for a few days…" Landon trailed off as Lucy buried her face into my chest. The sobs intensified, but it was the relieved kind. Landon and I exchanged a glance—one where I told him I'd take care of her, and he was free to go. He nodded, then moved down the long hallway to see his next patient while I held Lucy with promises that everything would be all right.

# Chapter 14
## Lucy

"LUCY..." The familiar voice tugged me out of the uncomfortable slumber. When I blinked, the world materialized around me, and I realized I had been stuck in this uncomfortable position for God knows how long. I'd definitely feel this later—in the worst way possible.

Luke was still beside me. I told him to go home—there was no reason for him to be here, especially when Ed was about to come in, too, but he told me to stop being ridiculous. He stuck by his word, and as the doctors approached us, I was glad he did.

My heart thudded in my chest. Despite what Landon told me, I was terrified that something would go wrong. My mom was the only family I had, and the thought of losing her made me feel like I was about to lose my mind.

The doctor who approached me wore blue scrubs as if he had just left the surgery. I quickly stood up, and Luke followed right away.

"Lucy Milburne?" he asked. I nodded. "Your mom is out of the surgery. It went as well as it possibly could have. We'll discuss her fall and what will need to be done later, but for now, I thought you may want to know she's stable."

"And her concussion?"

He pressed his lips into a thin line. "We'll know more when she wakes up, which should happen in about half an hour or so."

"Can I see her? Please?" I pleaded. Luke rubbed my back, still standing by my side.

"She's still out of it."

"That's fine. I need to see her to see for myself that she's alive." Tears threatened to flood my eyes again. I was sore all over, and I just wanted to see my mom. The doctor sighed before nodding once more. With a quick gesture, he indicated for us to follow, and I quickly marched behind him as he guided us to my mom's room.

Luke followed behind me, but he stopped in front of the room. "I'll give you some privacy," he told me. "I'll wait right here."

As the doctor opened the door, just like he mentioned, my mom was out of it, looking so peaceful in her slumber, like she didn't have a single worry on her mind—despite all the machines that surrounded her.

I reached for my mom's hand, giving it a light squeeze. My eyes welled up again. I should have been there to help her. How often did she do something like this on her own because I avoided returning to Port-Cartier? Guilt itched at me from inside.

My whole family was condensed into one person—my mom. And while I originally planned to stay here for two weeks, I knew now that I couldn't leave her when she needed me most. She'd need a lot of help with recovery, and I'd be damned if I wasn't there for it.

"You scared the shit out of me," I whispered, still holding her hand while her doctor checked out her vitals. "When you wake up, we're going to talk about this. You hear me?"

I didn't expect a response, but on some deeper level, I

knew she heard me. She was my mom. She always knew everything.

"You should go home and get some rest, Miss Milburne. You can see her in the morning." The doctor lingered at the door, gently prompting me to leave. I nodded weakly, heading back out where Luke was still waiting for me.

# Chapter 15
## Luke

LUCY LOOKED SLIGHTLY CALMER as she exited the room but was still visibly worried. It pained me to see her like this, and it was even worse to know there wasn't anything I could do to fix it.

"She'll be okay," I told her as the doctor gave us privacy again. "You Milburne ladies are strong." Lucy forced a small, exhausted smile to cross her face, but she didn't respond. A strand of curly hair drifted across her face, and I fought the urge to tuck it behind her ear.

"I'll drive you home. You should get some rest," I told her. She shook her head.

"I don't want to go home. It's going to be too silent. Too weird." Lucy pinched the bridge of her nose between her fingers, closing her eyes.

"Then you can come to stay with me. I know you wanted some space, but I agree, it would be best if you didn't stay alone." I wasn't stupid. I knew that after our kiss, she avoided me like the plague. Our meeting at the festival was purely coincidental. For the most part, I tried to respect her wishes, but right now, I figured it would be best if she were with someone. And I wasn't planning to make any moves or use this unfortunate situation for my own gain.

"Thank you, Luke. That'd be nice," she responded softly. For once, I was thankful she didn't fight me on this. We walked out of the hospital in silence and toward my truck.

Once I ensured she was inside and put on her belt, I shut the door and moved to the driver's seat. I let her lead any conversation she may want to have, but our surroundings remained silent aside from the soft hum of the radio. The stars were particularly prominent tonight, twinkling in the night sky. Port-Cartier had a low level of light pollution, so the view of the night sky was always spectacular. I wondered if she ever missed it.

When I turned to ask her about it, I found that her eyes were already closed, and her head leaned against the window. She was asleep. I wanted to soak in the sight for hours, but I forced myself to focus on the road before us, comfortable with the silence and the soft snores that echoed through my truck.

As I pulled up in front of my home, I contemplated waking her up, but ultimately, I decided against it. She needed to rest—today had been a long day for her. I moved as silently as I could as I exited the truck and then moved to the passenger's side. I wrapped my arms around her, scooping her in my embrace as I made my way up my front porch and into the house.

In moments like these, which, granted, didn't happen often, I wished I had come along further with my renovations. I didn't have any guest bedrooms finished yet, but that was okay. There was no way I was letting her sleep on the couch. As silently as I possibly could, I carried her to my bedroom, laying her down on my bed.

She stirred a little but didn't wake up.

I watched her sleep for a few seconds. Now that I wasn't driving, I could allow it.

Leaning down, I brushed the strand of her hair out of her

face, overcame by the sudden urge to kiss her. Just like I used to do a decade ago. Back then, not a single night we spent sleeping by each other's side ended without a kiss.

But I had yet to earn that privilege again, so instead, I tugged the blanket over her and let her get some rest.

Tonight, I'd be taking the couch.

# Chapter 16
## Lucy

AS I WOKE up this time, I was in a far more comfortable position. I was in an actual bed rather than a hospital chair, and I actually got a proper night's rest. In the far distance, I could hear the birds chirping, which momentarily distracted me from thoughts of my mom being in the hospital.

Luke's scent was prominent around me, to the point where it reclaimed my focus from the birds. I missed it and allowed myself another luxurious moment of inhaling his scent before I forced myself to sit up. The other side of the bed was untouched, which suggested that he didn't spend the night by my side.

I know that was to be expected, but a slight pang of disappointment spread through me regardless. Slowly, I made my way out of the bedroom and into the kitchen, where Luke was already making breakfast.

*Shirtless.*

I swallowed at the sight. His broad back was turned to me as he scrambled some eggs at the stove, humming an unfamiliar tune. With each movement, his muscular arms tensed. It was a sight for my sore eyes—one that momentarily distracted me from the chaos in my mind. When he turned, a smile popped on his lips.

"Good morning, Luce," he said.

"Morning." I rubbed my head. "What time is it?"

"Eleven a.m. I didn't want to wake you up. I figured you needed to rest properly."

"But my mom—"

"Landon called. Your mom woke up, and she's doing okay. Ed is with her. We can go see her once you eat."

I sat at a small kitchen island where three bar stools lined up, arching my brow. I tried to keep my eyes on him rather than on his bare chest, but the mission was only half-successful. "Bossy, aren't you?"

"Not bossy. Just taking care of you." He slid a plate across the marble counter. It had scrambled eggs, some fresh bread, bacon, and strawberries. Opening the fridge, he grabbed a carton of orange juice and poured me some, before he got to serving his plate.

"Thank you," I said quietly. "For everything. I don't even know how I would have gotten through last night without you." Even after a decade of separation, he was the first person I wanted by my side in a moment like that. Luke smiled. He didn't sit down beside me; instead, he nibbled on his breakfast from across the kitchen island.

"You don't have anything to thank me for. I only wish I could have helped more."

"You've already done enough," I pointed out, digging into my scrambled eggs. "Especially with a delicious breakfast like this." We ate breakfast mostly in silence. By the time I was nearly done with it, Luke started washing up the dishes. His back was turned toward me again, and I could stare at his physique. He only got more handsome over the past decade.

I wondered what it would be like to drag my hands down...

*No. What's wrong with you?* I scolded myself silently, stunned by the dirty thought.

"I was thinking you may want to shower before we head back to the hospital." His eyes traveled the length of my body sending shivers down my spine. "Last time you were here, I didn't return your clothes. I intended to, once I washed them, which I *did* do. So, at least you have something to wear." The back of my eyes burned at his words. He was so kind and so thoughtful, and I was so blessed to have him by my side right now. Any other scenario would have sucked. I would've been all on my own.

After I finished breakfast, I found myself in the bathroom and turned on the shower. As I stepped in, the hot water once again did wonders for my sore muscles and my worried mind. It was exactly what I needed. I leaned my back against the heated tiles, closing my eyes when unwanted thoughts snuck back into my mind.

I wondered what it would be like to sleep with Luke again after all these years. A decade spent away from each other would surely contain a lot of pent-up frustration. For the first time, I let myself acknowledge it was there. The frustration. The anger. The need. And there was nothing I could do about it...aside from wonder. In my mind, Luke was next to me in the shower, with his bare body pressed up against mine as he rammed himself inside me and—

No. No. I chewed my bottom lip, not allowing myself to lose another second in those filthy thoughts. He was kind to me because my mom was in a hospital, and I wasn't about to mistake it for anything else. Still, as I went to reach for his infamous three-in-one shower gel, I spotted another bottle right next to it. Vanilla. My favorite scent. Did he get it for me?

The smell was divine as I soaped myself up, relaxing further before washing it off my skin and stepping out of the shower. I quickly dried myself with a towel, only to also find a brand-new toothbrush and mouthwash at the side of the sink. He really was the kind of guy to think about everything.

Once I was all washed up and dressed, I got out of the bathroom. Luke was already waiting for me with his truck keys in his hand.

"Let's go see your mom."

# Chapter 17
## Luke

OUR DRIVE to the hospital was now much more lively. Lucy's mood picked up, and for a good reason—her mom is better. Landon didn't call. I called them and pestered them until I got an update on her mom, so I had good news when she woke up. Or that was, at least, what I told myself. After they insisted they couldn't give me details because I wasn't Eve's family, I called Landon, who had to call *them* and ask for updates. Still, it all worked out in the end because the smile on her face was more than worth it.

"I think I'm going to bake her some cookies the next time I visit her," she said, looking out the window as we headed toward Rockwood. "And I definitely have to make some for you. To thank you for everything."

"I already told you there's nothing to thank me for. You would've done the same for me." She *had* done the same for me. Lucy was there during the worst things to happen to me —save our breakup. We were dating when my grandpa passed away, and she didn't leave my side. Before we could continue the conversation, her phone buzzed, and she groaned as she looked at the caller ID.

"Who is it?" I asked.

"My ex," she grumbled. Every muscle in my body tensed. Why was he calling? Did he want her back? "Do you mind if I take this?"

"Not at all."

"Hello," she answered, and I lowered the radio volume so she could be uninterrupted during her call and so I could hear the words exchanged between them. I kept my eyes on the road.

"Hi, how are you?" he asked on the other side of the line.

"What do you want, Jason?"

"Shit, there's no need to be so cold to me, Luce." A surge of fury spread through me. Apparently, we shared a nickname for her, which annoyed me to no avail.

"You don't get to call me cold. You cheated on me for six months, so I'm sorry if I am less than cordial with you." Her volume rose with each syllable.

"Well, maybe if you weren't so fucking distant, I wouldn't have needed to do that. I needed you by my side, and you weren't there."

Was he seriously blaming *her* for cheating? The audacity of this asshole. I shook my head.

"Put that on speaker," I interrupted her. I was about to give this dickhead a piece of my mind.

"Who's that? Are you already fucking another guy, Lucy? I can't believe this!" her ex continued complaining on the other side of the line as she put me on speaker.

"You want to know who this is, and I'll tell you. I'm about to become your worst fucking nightmare if you ever speak to her like that again. She's not interested in anything you have to say about this charade of your affair, and she's most certainly not interested in being insulted and humiliated by you. So, the next time you speak to her, you show her some fucking respect. Or you'll regret the day you met her."

Lucy fell silent, and so did her ex. I didn't need to look at her to see how her mouth gaped.

"Now, say what you need to say, and leave her the hell alone."

He was still silent, so Lucy spoke up first. "What did you want, Jason?"

Jason then blew out a breath. "I need you to get your stuff out of the apartment."

"I'm not in town right now, and I'm dealing with a lot, so that's not going to happen. I'll check with Sailor to if she can help out and come pick up my things in a few days."

"I can't give you much time. Sarah moved in, and she wants your stuff out of here…so if you could make it happen sooner than later, I'd really appreciate it, Luce." It took every ounce of self-control I had not to send him to hell. Judging by Lucy's face, she felt the same way. She scrubbed at her face.

"Un-fucking-believable," she swore at him. I smiled. It wasn't like her to swear, but I was glad it was directed at this douche. "Fine, I'll make sure Sailor comes to pack all of my—"

"You won't need to pack anything. We already did it for you."

"Are you kidding me? We've been broken up less than two weeks, and you've already packed up my stuff and moved in with your mistress? You know what, Jason? You can go to hell!" She hung up with a puff.

"What a dick," she swore, and the initial swear was followed by a flood of more…interesting choices of words. Each suited her ex-boyfriend perfectly fine, from what I had heard. My hands were white with how tight I was gripping the steering wheel.

"I know it's not my place to ask, but I have to do it, Luce…" I said. "Did he always treat you like that? Because I'm about ready to hop on a plane to Seattle and give him a piece of my mind." And my fist right into his face. I was not a violent guy by any means, but someone talking to Lucy like that sent me into another kind of rage.

"He wasn't always like that. I guess it was about the time he started cheating when our relationship started to get rocky…and things took a turn for the worse. I thought it was just a bump on the road—something we could overcome. I thought it may be the stress about work…" With the way her voice broke, I momentarily gazed over at her. Her eyes welled up, and the sight of that alone made me want to beat the hell out of that guy.

"Hey, don't cry." I reached for her hand, giving her a small squeeze. She didn't pull back. "That guy doesn't deserve you."

Lucy sniffled. "That's not why I'm crying. I'm embarrassed about it all. How couldn't I have seen it coming?"

"Because you always see the best in people," I pointed out. "He's the asshole here. If he couldn't recognize what a great thing he had, that's on him. I regret every day that hasn't been spent with you."

"Luke," she said, squeezing my hand. "I can't do this right now."

"I know. I just…I want you to know it. So, you don't question yourself. Because trust me, this has nothing to do with you and everything to do with him. It's not your fault he cheated, and you didn't see it coming because you trusted him."

She sniffled. My gaze switched between the road ahead of us and her, but the tears were slowly disappearing, and I was pleased to see it.

"Still very good at comforting people," Lucy murmured, "if you weren't working at your dad's company, you should've been a therapist."

I laughed at her words. My hand remained locked around hers. "Well…I own the company now. Dad sold it to me last year when he decided to retire and spend more time with

Mom. I think it was the right move, but it's a lot of work between the company and renovating my home..."

"Wow, congratulations. Luke, that's amazing. I'm glad everything worked out for you..."

*Not everything,* I wanted to say, but I hoped that was about to change soon.

# Chapter 18
## *Lucy*

WHEN WE ARRIVED at the hospital, Ed was already in the lobby, and the state of his clothes suggested that he likely stayed the entire night. Something was going on between him and my mom—it was the only logical explanation for why he'd stay here overnight.

"Did you sleep here?" I asked him. Behind me, Luke handed over the coffee he had gotten for himself to Ed. He looked like he needed it more than us, and I more than appreciated the gesture.

"Yeah, I wanted to make sure Eve was okay throughout the night," Ed answered, taking the coffee with a grateful look. I fought the burn behind my eyes. I had felt so guilty over leaving Mom here alone, but it turned out she was in good company.

"Mom's lucky to have you." I hugged Ed, not letting him go for a few seconds. "Thank you for everything you do for her."

"You've got nothing to thank me for. She deserves the world," he said as he released me, and we headed into her room. This time, she was awake. *Thank God.* She still looked a little weak and shaken up, but to see her with her eyes open was the biggest relief.

"Mom!" I exclaimed, wrapping her in a hug. I couldn't help it. Tears began to fall. I had never been scared like this before.

"Oh, sweetie, don't cry. I'm fine."

"You're fine?" I hiccupped. "Look at you! Look at your leg! And they said you may even have a concussion!"

"I'll be up and going in no time," she assured me, but I highly doubted that was the case. I was there for the fall. It looked serious, and I figured it would take her a while to recover.

"Have you talked with the doctor? Do you know when you'll be getting out of here?"

"Well, the good thing is the doctor's right here to talk to you," another voice said from the door. I turned my head to see Landon. He was Luke's brother and one of the reasons why I believed my mom was in good hands. He was good at what he did; that was a well-known fact in our town.

"Landon," I said, "thank God you're here."

He smiled. "That's my job, Lucy. I ensured your mom was in the best hands possible and checked up on her regularly." He gave Luke a strange look, but I didn't question any of it— as long as my mom was cared for.

"The leg will take a while to heal. You'll have to use crutches and keep the movement to a minimum. If you overdue it the longer your recovery will be. The break was bad, but we've managed to—"

"How long?" my mom interrupted Landon impatiently, crossing her arms over her chest.

"Eve…you're going to have to take it slow for a while," Ed reminded her, placing his hand on her shoulder.

"I have a business to run!"

"Well, your business is going to have to wait. You'll need to keep weight off of it for at least a month and a half, and we're going to implement physical therapy to slowly get you back to walking. All in all, it will be a few months before…"

Landon didn't even finish his words before my mom began shaking her head. "Absolutely not. It's just me at my flower store. Taking on someone new will take some time and I need to train them and—oh, God. What am I going to do? I have to work!"

"Mom, you have me," I pointed out.

"Yes, but you're leaving in a week."

I gave my mom a look. "I'm on summer break, so I can extend my time here until I need to return to work. I can be here for at least six more weeks. When I was younger, I was by your side at that store day and night. I picked up a thing or two. It's the least I can do for now, and we'll see how it goes from there."

"Are you sure, sweetie?"

"Of course. We're family; that's what family does. I'm not going to leave you now when you need me the most." I looked up at Ed. "Ed can't do everything on his own, you know."

My mom looked at Landon again. "And when can I go home?" she asked him.

"I'd like to keep you until tomorrow morning just to make sure there are no complications, and then you'll be free to go," Landon explained. "This goes without saying, but you won't be able to go up and down the stairs for a while." The same panicked look returned to my mom's face, but I did what I could to ease it.

"Of course. We'll set up the guest room for you down-stairs. You don't have to worry about anything, Mom. We'll have everything sorted out." I met Ed's eyes. "Can you stay with mom a little longer? I want to head back home to sort everything out for her arrival and bring her stuff downstairs as soon as possible."

Luke stepped beside me. "I'll come with you to help out."

Just when I thought he couldn't possibly do more for me, he did. He was there in every way I needed him, and I wasn't sure I'd ever be able to repay him any of this.

"Okay, we're going to head out and sort everything out around the house." I kissed my mom on the cheek. "All you need to do is sit still."

My mom gestured toward her leg with a mischievous smile. "I wasn't planning on going anywhere, sweetheart."

"And don't give Landon or the nurses too much trouble." This time, she laughed. The sound relieved me, and I knew she'd be back to her old, usual self in no time.

As Luke and I headed out, I was already in full planning mode.

"Okay, I'll need to let Sailor know that I won't be back until the end of August. My car is parked at the airport; maybe I can get her to move it somewhere for me. I also need

more clothes. I'll need to learn Mom's system for her floral shop. I mean, I know a thing or two about her arrangements, but surely she's updated her system since the last time I was there…" Had that not been a decade ago, maybe I would've been more familiar with it. Guilt threatened to itch at me all over again, but I refused to let it happen. I was going to help my mom get through this.

# Chapter 19
## Luke

WHEN WE STOPPED at the gas station, I knew I had to do something to make this easier on her. I'd seen the look on her face last night—Lucy was terrified of losing her mom, and she seemed even more terrified now that she'd somehow let her down.

That wasn't going to happen, not under my watch. After I filled up my tank, I pulled my phone out as I waited to pay.

ME: Hey everyone, Eve fell and broke her leg. She won't be able to put weight on it for a while, so Lucy plans to stay to help her out. I've just been with her at the hospital. We're heading back to her home now. if you're free and able to help adjust the home for Lucy's mom, feel free to stop by.

MOM: Oh my God

MOM: Is she okay?

LOGAN: obviously not mom

LOGAN: unfortunately for her…and more fortunately for Luke Puke

MOM: Don't call your brother that

I rolled my eyes, unwilling to engage in any more of their nonsense once it was my turn to pay for the gas. I also grabbed one of Lucy's favorite chocolate bars. It was peanut-flavored. Or, at least, it *was* her favorite a decade ago. Back then, she claimed peanuts were the superior nuts. I hoped her stance remained.

As I hopped back into my truck, I handed over the chocolate bar to her. Instantly, she smiled. "You remembered…"

"Of course. A guy can never forget multiple lectures about peanuts by his first love…"

She laughed loudly, opening up the packaging and taking a bite. Lucy offered me one, too, but I shook my head as I started the car. While peanuts earned some points for being her favorite, I still wasn't willing to eat them.

The rest of the ride was silent until we arrived at her mom's home. A few cars were already in the driveway. She turned toward me with a confused look.

"I called in reinforcements to help," I explained. "I hope that's okay."

She launched herself at me, encasing me in a hug. I didn't waste any time pulling her in close. Her scent snuck into my nostrils, and I closed my eyes briefly. I was almost able to pretend she was still mine.

As unfortunate as Eve's fall was, though, one good thing came out of it. Lucy would stay here longer, which meant I also had a chance to win her back. I wouldn't mess it up this time because this was the woman I wanted to spend the rest of my life with. And I refused to let a single day pass without me proving it to her.

"Thank you, Luke," she said into my neck.

"Anything for you, Luce."

A sharp rap sounded on my window, and then Logan's annoying face interrupted our moment. "Are you two going to spend all day in there, or are you going to come help?"

I pulled back, and Lucy's cheeks reddened as she smiled at me. "We should probably go before Logan tries to jump on the truck."

Landon was working, so he wasn't here, but my parents and my annoying brother came along to help. Lucy's face lit up the moment she exited the truck, and she dashed toward them.

"Mr. and Mrs. Everett! It's so nice to see you again!" she beamed, and both my parents pulled her into a hug. It was like staring into my past all over again. So many times, they told me Lucy was the daughter they never had. They were heartbroken when we broke up and even more hurt when Lucy just vanished, even if they understood the reasoning behind it.

"Sweetie, how many times have we told you that you can call us by our first names?" my mom said. "And we were so sorry to hear about your mother."

"Sorry, old habits die hard," Lucy apologized. Logan stood by me, elbowing me suggestively. I fought the urge to roll my eyes. "Linda, Levi, how have you been? And thank you so much for coming here today. It means more than you can imagine."

"Of course, darling," my mom continued, "we're good now that we're both retired. Although, if Levi doesn't find a hobby soon, I may send him back to work."

Lucy let out a belly laugh. "I'm so happy for you two. You deserve all the rest now that you're retired. You've worked so hard for so long."

"Alright, enough chit-chat!" I slapped my hands together. My mom tended to talk...a lot, and my dad had an even worse habit of not interrupting her. If I didn't end this, it could drag long into the night. "Time to get things done."

96

# Chapter 20
## Lucy

I STAYED BEHIND as Luke's family entered my mom's home, giving him a nervous glance.

"Do you think they still like me?" I asked silently. I did disappear without a word at the point when they were practically my second family. My mom told me they kept asking about me all the time, but I didn't have the strength to connect with anyone in this town back then.

"Luce, what are you talking about?" Luke said, arching his brow. "They've known you for years."

"They've known me a decade ago. But since then…" I trailed off. "Also, I was your girlfriend back then. And now I'm not anymore."

Luke placed his hand on my lower back. It was likely meant to be reassuring, but instead, it sent an electrifying spark through my entire body.

"You're being ridiculous. You're impossible not to like," Luke said as he rubbed my back.

*"What is it?" Luke asked me as I stepped on his front porch. I wore a floral dress—one that my mom loved the most. It seemed like a perfect fit for a night like this—when a girl would finally be introduced to her boyfriend's parents.*

*"I'm just…nervous. Do you think they'll like me?"*

*"Luce, they love you. They've known you your whole life."*

*"Well…yes," I murmured. They did. But I supposed things changed when a girl started to date someone's son. Levi and Linda wanted the best for their boys, just like my mom wanted the best for me. I only hoped they'd see I wanted to be nothing less than that. "But this is different."*

*"No," he breathed, leaning forward to give me a peck on my lips. "It's not different at all." The door opened before we could knock, and we quickly pulled back from each other. My cheeks burned with embarrassment as his mother stood there with a warm smile. She didn't mind catching us amidst affection the slightest bit. She pulled me into a hug right away.*

*"Lucy, come on in! We're so excited to have you for dinner. I made homemade lasanga. I hope you're up for it!"*

*"Thank you, Mrs. Everett. And of course. I've heard nothing but praise for your lasanga."*

*"Please, call me Linda. You already know everyone, so I don't need to make*

*introductions. Make yourself at home while I finish up dinner." His mom looked at Luke.*

*"You're in charge of making sure she's comfortable," she told him before she bustled off to the kitchen.*

*"See, I told you they would like you," Luke whispered in my ear. As we got in, his father was the second one to greet me.*

*"You've heard my wife. I want to go by my first name and nothing else," he said as he gave me a light pat on the shoulder. I couldn't stop smiling. I already felt so comfortable when his two brothers came in, too. There was definitely no need for introduction there; I practically grew up with them as much as I grew up with Luke.*

*Sitting at the dinner table, I couldn't help but feel a little envious. I had known his family for years, as is common in small towns, but being welcomed into their home and experiencing their love firsthand was different. Coming from a small, quiet*

*household with just me and my mom, this boisterous and loving family was a stark*

*contrast to what I was used to. I found myself falling in love with them all the same.*

"Earth to Lucy Goosey?" Logan said, waving a hand in front of my face.

"I'm sorry I didn't catch that; what did you say?" I asked, breaking out of my daydream. Luke's and my exchange at the front porch had somehow dragged me in yet another memory.

"We moved a few things from Eve's bedroom downstairs, but we're unsure what else

to bring down. Can you show us what you would like?"

"Sure, follow me." I nodded, making a small gesture with my hand.

For the better portion of the afternoon, we rearranged the guest bedroom to make it easy for her mom to get around. We also brought in most of her things from upstairs and the little knick-knacks I knew my mom would want around. My mom always liked things in a particular way, and I wanted to make this transition as easy for her as possible.

"Sweetheart," Linda said as she pulled me aside while the guys readjusted the bed's location in the bedroom. "I've pulled some simple frozen meals from my freezer and brought them over. I popped them in your freezer instead. I figured you'd want to help out your mom as much as possible, and the last thing I want you to be thinking about is cooking. I'll bring in some fresh meals, too…these are just for the emergency occasions."

I struggled to hold back tears, my eyes blinking rapidly as I embraced Linda. "I can't express how much this means to me," I whispered, my voice choking with emotion. This was a rare occurrence in the city. One of the things I always yearned for in Seattle was this sense of community. When life took a turn for the worse, the people in town were always the first to lend a helping hand. And their support meant more than any words could describe.

"Sweetheart, there's no need to cry. It's the least we can do."

"It's…not that," I admitted, sniffling as I pulled back. "It's just…I'm sorry for disappearing. I never meant to hurt you and leave—"

Linda shook her head. "There's absolutely no need to apologize, sweetheart. You did what you thought was best, and no one can blame you." She gave me a small smile. "Right now, we're all just glad to have you back." She looked at Luke, who was bickering with Logan about the most convenient position for the dresser. "Luke especially."

The Everetts stayed for dinner after helping me with everything—which, for tonight, was pizza from the nearby restaurant. Ed shot me a text to let me know he was still with my mom and that she was feeling better, so any of the remains of the guilt dispersed, and I let myself fully enjoy their company until it was time for them to leave.

Luke was the last one at my home. I walked him out to his truck, pulling my hands around my slender frame as a light breeze swung around me.

"I can't thank you and your family enough for everything," I told him.

"You don't need to thank me. That's what we do for those we care about." I smiled up at him. His eyes sparkled in the lights of the porch. "Do you think you'll be okay with staying alone tonight? You can come to my place if you'd like. And I promise you, it's definitely not a booty call."

I laughed, shaking my head. "I appreciate the offer and the clarification, but I think I'll be fine." And for once, I meant it. Things have been so hectic lately, but now that I knew my mom would be okay and that the ghost of my first relationship no longer haunted me, I could be on my own. We fell silent momentarily, and then Luke's gaze dropped to my lips.

"I want to kiss you right now, Luce, but we need to talk before we muddy the waters anymore. I want to do this right."

His words struck me, but I nodded anyway. The weirdest part was I *wanted* him to kiss me. But he was right; we needed to talk properly. Luke brushed back a piece of my hair that had escaped from my bun before leaning in and kissing my forehead.

"I'll stop by tomorrow." Luke hopped in his truck but didn't leave until I had closed the door. For once, I thought things may be all right after all. There was only one more thing to handle for tonight.

ME: Hey, can I ask you for a favor?

SAILOR: Of course! What do you need?

ME: Could you pick up my things from Jason's apartment? He's packed all my stuff so Sarah could move in.

ME: I was planning on coming back in a little over a week and doing it myself, but that's apparently inconvenient for him…and then things changed because my mom broke her leg, and I'll be staying here a few more weeks

SAILOR: Are you fucking kidding me? Of course, I'll pick up your stuff. It'll give me a chance to give him a piece of my mind.

SAILOR: How is Eve doing? Please tell her that I miss her and wish her a speedy recovery!!

ME: she'll be okay. she's just worried about her business, so I want to stay and help

ME: P.S. She definitely has a boyfriend.

SAILOR: Eve was always a wild card ;)

ME: Please…don't. Anyway, be good, and thank you. I'll let you know what happens with Mom.

SAILOR: Okay, I love you girly-pop.

# Chapter 21
## Lucy

THE NEXT MORNING, I was up before the sun, which said something because I was not a morning person. Still, I wanted everything to be perfect for my mom. I took a shower and got dressed, quickly making some pancakes that I could later reheat for my mom, too. Hospital food has never been much, and that woman always had the appetite of a lion, so I figured she'd be hungry once she got home.

Around eight in the morning, Ed pulled up and helped my mom get out of the car. She had crutches with her but could not fully support her body, so he carried her bridal style. I couldn't help but smile.

"I bet you never imagined this was why Ed would carry you like this," I said teasingly, enjoying how my mom's cheeks reddened at my words. She quickly looked away, and Ed didn't stop grinning for a second.

"Let's get you settled in," Ed said as he headed into the guest room. I followed behind them.

"I tried to make everything as accessible as possible. The guys have even brought your TV here, so you don't need to move around much."

"Thank you," my mom said. "I couldn't stay in that damn hospital for a moment longer."

"That's true," Ed confirmed. "She drove them insane to the point where they released her early."

"Sounds like my mom..." I gave a small chuckle. "Anyway, are you guys hungry? I made some pancakes."

"I'd love to stay, and I appreciate the offer, but I've got to get back to work," Ed said. I nodded.

"Of course. Thank you for everything; I got it from here." I gave his arm a small pat. I couldn't thank him enough for everything he had done for my mom. He hesitated momentarily before leaning down, kissing my mom for a second—if that. Ed quickly pulled back, as if he had been caught doing something illegal, and then left. I didn't stop smiling as I stared at my mom.

"Is there anything you want to tell me?" I arched my brow.

"Well..."

"Relax, Mom. I know you two have been dating. I suspected it since I first came here. Now...how about I bring you some breakfast?" My mom nodded eagerly, and I returned to the kitchen to retrieve everything I had prepared. Pancakes, fresh fruit, orange juice. Just the way she liked it. I brought everything in on a tray.

"I feel like I've been run over by a truck," my mom groaned, "but this is going to help." My nerves were still shot from her accident, but I was glad to have her home and I was going to do everything I could to make her comfortable.

I smiled sympathetically.

"I figured we should get some food into you, and then I'll give you some of your pain meds." Mom nodded, digging into her food. With how happily she ate it, one would think she hadn't eaten in ages. The doorbell rang when I was about to steal a strawberry from her plate.

"Saved by the bell." I smirked as I opened the door, only

to find Luke holding a tray of coffees in one hand and flowers in the other. My brows furrowed.

"Where did you get the flowers?" I asked him. "My mom's store is shut…"

"Morning, Luce," Luke said, holding one of the coffees out to me. "And a gentleman doesn't kiss and tell, sweetheart, unless you *want* to kiss me."

My cheeks burned, but I tried to redirect my focus. "Thank you. I could use another boost of coffee this morning." I took it eagerly. No matter how much I searched for the perfect coffee in Seattle, nothing could ever compare to Brew Haha. "I'm going to be lost without Brew Haha when I return to Seattle at the end of the summer."

Luke eyed me momentarily before he shook his head and cleared his throat. Only then did the situation I put him in dawn upon me. A part of me wondered if he also shared the dirty thoughts I occasionally caught myself thinking about him.

"How's your mom doing today?" He swiftly changed the topic.

"She's eating breakfast right now. She said she feels like she's been run over by a

truck. Once she's done eating, I'll give her more pain meds. Do you want to say hi? I'm sure she would like the company."

"Sure, I also brought her coffee, but I wasn't sure if she could have it."

"Well, the doctors didn't mention any dietary restrictions, so I'm sure it's fine." I led the way into the guest room, where my mom was nearly done with her breakfast. Her expression brightened when she saw Luke in the doorway.

"Lukey, you brought coffee. Thank God! I wasn't about to say anything, but Lucy forgot about my morning coffee." As Luke approached, he handed over her coffee. How did he even know what she got? "You were always my favorite boyfriend of Lucy's."

"Mom!" I scolded, and Luke grinned with a shrug.

"What? I never did like Jason, and see how that turned out?" My mom took a sip of her coffee. "I told you that boy was trouble, but you didn't believe me!"

I covered my face. I couldn't believe Mom had said that. On second thought, I could

believe it. It sounded *exactly* like my mom. Instead of focusing on the burning embarrassment in my cheeks, I switched my attention to the coffee Luke brought over and how it awoke my taste buds.

"Oh, don't feel bad, Luce." Luke rubbed my back. Again, every cell in my body reacted. I wasn't sure if it was just everything we had been through together recently, or if I never fully got over him, but the more these innocent touches he gave me, the more I craved. A part of me even regretted pulling back from that kiss at his place.

"Okay, I'm leaving you to handle your visit alone," I said, pointing to Luke before I looked at my mom. "Mom, let me know when you're done and if you need help getting to the bathroom."

I walked out of the room, ready to tackle the dishes from this morning. While I knew they were joking around, Luke's presence increased the burning in my body, and I just needed a moment away from him.

"Hey," Luke said only a few minutes later, bringing Mom's breakfast dishes. I jumped at the sudden tone, nearly dropping my coffee into the sink.

"Shit." I placed the coffee on the counter beside me, trying to recollect my composure. Why was it suddenly so hard to keep my cool around him?

"I didn't mean to scare you." Luke plopped the dishes into the sink, offering a small smile. I returned it.

"You didn't, I mean, you did—but I was so zoned out that I didn't hear you walk in."

"Is everything okay?" Concern etched his face.

"Yeah, I just…I didn't sleep well. I had a few nightmares, and then I was overthinking how I'm going to help mom at her flower store. It will be a lot of work, but I want her to rest as much as possible," I admitted. "You know her. She'll want to be on her feet constantly, which will definitely delay her recovery." I returned to washing the dishes. Luke stood behind me, and then his hands found my shoulders. He moved slowly, circularly, hitting all the right spots and sending tingles through my whole body.

"God," I moaned, relaxing my entire body under his firm touch. "That feels good. You're really good at this."

"Thanks, I dated a woman who was a masseuse." He grinned behind me.

"Can you give me her number? I'll date her if I can get massages like this." I groaned again, sinking further into the massage. Luke chuckled, but it was deeper this time, as was the intensity of his touch. He found a few knots in my back that desperately needed to be released.

"I should go into my mom, but I don't want this to stop. Can you follow me around

today?" I asked.

"That wouldn't be weird at all." Luke laughed, sweeping over my back once more in a strong, circular motion. His body was closer to mine, too. I could practically feel him brush up against me, just as I could feel the hardened bulge in his pants. I knew I shouldn't have done it, but I found myself pushing back against him before fully comprehending what was happening. His hands were on my back, his hips against me, and his lips dangerously close to my neck. We were playing with fire, and neither of us was strong enough to pull back, even if we got burned. Until…

"Lucy!" my mom called out, and we moved away from each other quickly.

"Coming in a second!" I responded. My gaze locked on Luke as I turned around to face him. He swallowed.

"Hey…I know the flower shop isn't open today, but maybe I could come help you out tomorrow. I mean…an extra pair of hands doesn't hurt, does it?"

"You're right," I said, even if I couldn't fully grasp his words right now. I would've agreed to anything he said. "I've got to go check on my mom, but I'll…see you tomorrow, then?"

Luke nodded, lingering in his spot for a moment longer before he headed out, and I went to check up on my mom. The hospital had given her crutches to use, which had made it easier for her to get around. The trick was not to put them close to her, or she would be up and moving around even though the doctor had said she needed to take it easy and not put any weight on her leg.

After helping her to the bathroom, I got her back to the bed.

"Would it be okay to keep the shop closed tomorrow, too? So that I can get a hang of everything. And Luke will come to help me, too."

My mom smiled knowingly. "Sure, sweetheart. That's more than fine."

The doorbell rang again, and I knew the day would be full of visitors.

And I was right. By the end of the day, I was pretty sure that everyone in Port-Cartier had come to visit her.

# Chapter 22
## Lucy

THE NEXT MORNING, I peeked into the guest bedroom, only to find my mom still sleeping. Ed was already here, sipping on his coffee in the kitchen.

"Morning," I greeted him, offering a smile. "I'm heading into the shop. I don't want to wake her up. Do you happen to know where she keeps her keys?"

"Of course, Luce," Ed responded. *Luce.* My smile was beyond my control, now widening further. I couldn't help but wonder how long my mom had been with him that he picked up on the nickname, too. I'm happy for them; he's good for her. Ed pulled out her ring of keys, already knowing where they were located.

"Everything you need should be in the office. Your mom usually has me help out with the flower delivery when I can —it should be in two days, but she starts preparing the day earlier. You'll need to pick through the flowers, write them off, and dispose of them," he told me. "I know that she has her notes on her desk…but anything else, you'll have to ask her when she wakes up."

"Thank you, Ed. This means a lot." I'd call my mom later —for now, I just wanted to get a hang of as many things as possible on my own. I found that it was the best way to immerse myself into the business. Plus, I wanted to bother my mom as little as possible. She deserved to recover properly. I worked for her during high school, so I was sure some things had changed in the ten years I'd been gone, but I figured I'd understand the general drift of the shop.

When I got to the shop, though, I realized nothing had changed. The sight was *just* as I remembered it. The exterior of the building was still painted in the same pale peach shade, and the vintage sign that read 'Blushing Blooms' remained unchanged. Inside were endless wooden shelves lined with colorful vases holding various kinds of flowers. The large windows allowed plenty of sunlight in, which benefited my mom's business. In the back of the shop were two smaller rooms—one that my mom used as her office and the other that held no particular purpose other than for her to invite people in occasionally. More flowers, a mismatched sofa and armchair, and an antique little coffee table. Growing up, it was one of my favorite spots where Luke and I would spend a lot of time together, making out when my mom was out delivering flowers and I was in charge of the shop.

The office was just as chaotic; my mom was still hand-writing everything, including all orders, stock taking, and business expenses. It was a mess of endless papers and stacks

of sticky notes with orders for each day. This was going to be a lot…to go through.

When Luke came in, he brought in coffee from Brew Haha, and I appreciated it more than he knew as I greeted him with a smile.

"You're god sent," I told him, taking a sip. "It will take me ages to get through everything. My mom…how does she even function? Nothing is digitalized. She's probably losing so much of her time because of this."

Luke reached forward, brushing a strand of my hair behind my ear. My teeth sunk into my bottom lip as I watched him. "Well, this may be the time to help her out. You could implement a new system. You're keeping the shop closed today, and I'll be with you all day so we can figure out what can be done."

"All day?" I shook my head. "Luke, I can't ask that of you. You have your own business to take care of—"

"That's the beauty of being my own boss," he assured me. "I dictate my hours. And I'd rather spend them by your side."

"I...." I trailed off. There was a lot I wanted to say. A lot that he was doing for me. Where was it all leading? What were we doing? Aside from worrying about my mom's business, endless questions roamed through my mind about us—about what we could be.

"I told you we needed to talk. I know this isn't the ideal time, but I no longer want to beat around the bush. I want to be with you. And before you start shaking your head, let me explain. When I saw you at your welcome home surprise party, I knew I was not going to let you go this time."

"Luke, you broke up with me last time. I know ten years have passed, but what's changed? We both have lives now..."

"I was an idiot. I fucked up. You were going to sacrifice yourself by going to college with me, and I didn't want that for you. If I broke up with you, I thought it would allow you to go to the college you wanted."

Tears streamed down my face. Was this really the reason why he broke up with me? After all these years, I had never gotten closure. And now, he was finally giving it to me. The only question was if it would be enough for me to reopen that chapter. "You know what, you *are* an idiot. You should have talked to me. We could have figured something out. Breaking up with me shouldn't have been your first choice."

"You're right." He stepped closer to me. One of his hands found my hip, and this time, I didn't pull back in any way. "It shouldn't have. Back then, I didn't know what I was doing. Now I do. I was a scared kid who didn't want to hold you back from your dreams. Now, I'm a man ready to fight for what he wants." His familiar scent hit my nostrils. I closed my eyes, and memories instantly flooded me. Hard and fast, all at once. The first kiss under the bleachers at the high school football game, sneaking out to meet each other late at night, the countless conversations about our future together.

I couldn't deny my feelings for him anymore. I tried so hard to move on, but my heart reminded me of what it truly needed every time. And it had always been him.

I couldn't tell how this was going to end. I couldn't tell if I had a future here, but right now, all I knew was that I needed to be closer to him. As my eyes opened, I leaned up, pressing my lips against his. He eagerly greeted my kiss, and we were both struck by the passion and spark we still shared.

I didn't expect this. I came to my mom's shop to handle her business, yet I found myself stumbling backward toward the small lounge area in the back. I thanked God that the 'CLOSED' sign was displayed because the last thing I wanted was to be interrupted.

"I've been thinking about this for days," Luke whispered against my lips. His hands trailed up my chest, popping open button by button of my blouse. I shuddered beneath his touch already.

"Luke…" I whimpered with need. I wasn't strong enough to fight this attraction anymore. And I didn't want to. I wanted to surrender to it in every way there was.

He collared my neck while his other hand drifted lower now that he was done unbuttoning my blouse, sneaking underneath my skirt. I was pinned against the wall, with his fingers brushing against the lace of my panties and his hot mouth a breath away from mine.

"Are you wet for me?"

I nodded softly. That pleased him, apparently, because his fingers slipped beneath the thin lace, settling between my folds and brushing over my clit. I let out a little gasp.

"Just as I suspected. Good girl" Again, no words could make it past my lips, so I nodded desperately, spreading my legs open for him wider. I rolled my hips toward him, eager for any friction. "How needy of you, Luce…needing me to pleasure this sweet pussy of yours." *The mouth of this man*, I thought to myself. He had a heart of gold and a mouth of filth, and I loved every second of it.

In one quick motion, he flipped us around, and I landed on the small sofa with him on top of me. Somehow, his hand remained against my pussy the entire time—now, circling my clit and applying pressure where I needed it the most.

But I needed more.

I needed him in me now.

"Please," I breathed, tipping my head back.

"Please, what?" he asked, still playing with my clit. It was driving me insane.

"Please, I need you inside me," I begged. I wasn't above begging if it got me what I wanted.

"Take off your bra. I want to see all of you," Luke demanded as he hiked up my skirt and yanked my panties down my legs. I squirmed on the sofa and unhooked my bra, releasing my breasts. "That's a good girl." He reached for my left breast, toying with my nipple, before paying the same attention to the right one, too.

"Now, I have question. Can you be quiet so that I can worship this pussy?" I nodded again, unable to form words. He lowered himself between my thighs. Just the sight of him there was nearly enough to make me come. "Don't make me repeat myself."

"Yes, I can be quiet," I gasped, and Luke didn't waste a moment as he dove in. He licked down my folds, and I could barely hold in a moan.

"Oh God," I whispered.

"I want my name on your lips the next time you speak," he demanded, flickering his tongue against my clit. I bit my lip to stay silent—as he requested, but I'd never been the one to be quiet in bed, and it was killing me right now. Luke shifted as he slid a finger through my folds to my entrance. He circled my entrance, not quite letting it slide in yet. I was going out of my mind with need.

"Please, Luke," I panted, and he rewarded me by letting his fingers join his tongue. I was so wet that he met no resistance.

"You're so fucking wet for me," he moaned. "I've been dreaming about this pussy for days." He added another finger, stretching me slightly and preparing me for his cock. Because I needed to have it—otherwise, I may lose my sanity.

"Oh fuck, Luke. Just like that," I moaned, barely keeping my voice quiet. I wasn't going to last long like this, and he knew it. With each passing second, I was getting closer to that point of no return, choking on my breath and shaking against his touch. He continued his pace, taking all of me and giving me no choice but to take it.

By the time he finally allowed the third finger to join, I shattered into a million pieces. In one move, he straddled me and smothered my moan with his mouth. He kissed me fervently while still using his fingers. My orgasm barreled on like a freight train; I couldn't tell if it was one long one or if one ended and another began. My legs shook, and I tried to close them as I finished, but Luke kept them spread open for him.

When he didn't allow me to do that, I reached for his pants, unbuckling his belt and unzipping the zipper to reveal his hardened cock. I meant it when I said it. I needed him inside me.

# Chapter 23
## Luke

I COULD BARELY PROCESS what was happening, but it felt right. It was exactly what I needed. For so long, I yearned for this moment. I wanted her more than anything else in this world, and now that I was finally getting her, I was never letting her go.

"God, you taste so good," I murmured against her lips as she unleashed my cock. It was so hard as it ached for her need, covered in precum as she gave it one long stroke. I grunted, pushing myself into her hand, when I suddenly realized…

"I don't have anything." I swore at myself for coming here unprepared. It wasn't like I expected this to happen. "I haven't been with anyone in a long time, and I…"

"I'm on birth control," was all she whispered as she pushed her hips upward. *Fuck.* I nearly came right there and then. My cock hooked at her entrance as I straightened up on top of her, getting rid of my shirt and tossing it on the floor before. Finally, I allowed myself to slide deep inside her.

And I was home.

She was warm, and wet, and so fucking right, that I questioned my entire life. How the hell did I go so long without this? Without her?

"Luke!" she whimpered again, arching herself underneath me. Every time I thrusted back inside her, she clenched around me. Her eyes rolled back into her head as she drew in a shaky breath.

"Fuck, you feel so good. I've missed being inside you," I purred, watching her take me. It was as if her pussy was created for me. "You're so fucking pretty when you take me." With a moment of hesitation, she looked down. Both our gazes were stuck at the spot where we connected. My hand found her throat, applying slight pressure there as I pounded myself into her. My hands trembled as much as her legs did; every muscle in my body was tense.

Lucy had always been the most beautiful woman in the world for me, but seeing her like this awoke something primal inside me.

"Tell me how much you like this cock inside you, Luce," I demanded. The sofa squeaked beneath us as I moved on top of her, taking what was mine. All of her was mine—every breath, every whimper, every little sound she made.

"It feels so good...oh God Luke!" My name came an octave higher than she likely expected, and while I appreciated her pleasure, the last thing I wanted was for someone to hear this. I shut her up with another kiss, quickening my pace. I was dangerously close to my orgasm.

"You're such a good girl, Luce, taking my cock like this." She nodded frantically, and I rewarded her by applying some pressure to her clit with my thumb. That did it for her. In a matter of seconds, she began trembling violently again as pleasure struck her, and I followed closely behind, only lasting a few more thrusts before I spilled myself inside her.

"Fuck!" I grunted, lingering on top of her. My body refused to move, even after I had come, just wanting to soak in her presence, before I finally managed to plop on the sofa, pulling her into my arms. We stayed like that for a little while, enjoying the comfortable silence until she broke it.

"You've got a filthy mouth. I'd hate to think you kiss your mother with those lips."

A loud laugh escaped my lips. "Well, you're the one to blame. You bring it out of me."

"Sure…sure. It's always easiest to blame others." She nudged me, smiling up at me. I tightened my embrace around her.

"Well…being in between your thighs did something primal to me. I could hardly think." Lucy's cheeks reddened, and she quickly looked away, biting her bottom lip. Something was on her mind. "What is it?"

"Nothing, it's just…I've never experienced someone wanting to go down on me so…. enthusiastically," she admitted. A pang of jealousy spread through me, but I fought it. I couldn't change what had happened, but I could make sure I was the only man to be there for as long as we both lived. And I had every intention of doing that.

"Trust me when I tell you this. Being there is all I ever want to do. But…unfortunately"—I gestured around us—"we have things we've got to do."

After we both recovered and got dressed, I went to get lunch from the local sandwich bar. It opened well after Lucy left, but I knew she would love it, regardless. The door opened with the usual 'ding' as I entered with two sandwiches and their famous mint lemonade.

"Lunch is here, sweetheart," I called out. I expected her at the front—since she said she wanted to keep track of the inventory, but she was nowhere to be found. "Sweetheart?" I repeated, heading to the back of the store.

Luce was in the office, though she looked like she had seen a ghost. She was entirely pale, breathing heavily. I quickly dropped the paper bag with lunch on the desk, approaching her.

"Hey, what's going on?" I asked her. Instantly, my mind was considering all the worst options. Had she gotten some bad news? Hurt herself?

"Panic...attack," Luce managed to muster, her hands shaking as she stared at me. She reminded me of a wild animal who had just been trapped. I nodded, dragging a chair in front of her.

"Sit down. Put your head between your knees." She did as I asked but continued to struggle to breathe. "Take deep breaths for me," I instructed her, placing my hand on her back. It pained me to see her like this, but the best thing I could do was guide her through this. "And one more," I repeated. Her breathing grew steadier, and her muscles relaxed beneath my hand.

"Sorry about that," she said once she stopped shaking. I reached into the bag, handing her the lemonade. Her brows furrowed as she looked up at me. I shrugged.

"I wish I had some water, but that's all I can give you now. You'll love it." As she took the first sip, I knew I was right. Her face showed it. "And there's nothing to apologize for, Luce. But I would like to know what happened."

"I just got overwhelmed. When I first walked in, I saw how...messy it all was, but I guess I didn't anticipate how hard it would be until I started going through all the sticky notes. I started freaking out, thinking I couldn't do this, and before I knew it, I was in the middle of a panic attack."

"Do you have panic attacks a lot?" Concern etched my face, and guilt pounded inside me at the thought of her going through this countless times before without me around.

"I suppose so. They usually pop up when I'm stressed or under a lot of pressure. To be honest with you, I'm surprised the first one hasn't happened earlier." She rubbed her forehead. "It started when I was in college. But it's fine...I can handle it. I always figure it out. I just...I saw the state of my mom's office and her organizational system—or lack thereof —and it sent me into a tailspin. I'm worried I can't do this. I'm worried I'll fail. My mom is depending on me. This is her livelihood, and I could mess it all up." She looked like panic was rising inside her again, so I lightly rubbed her shoulder to soothe her. "I already left her once, Luke. I can't mess this up again. She trusts me."

"Listen to me. If anyone can do this, it's you," I told her firmly. She took another sip of the lemonade, shaking her head.

"How do you know?" she asked. "I've only just come back. You...you don't know me like you used to."

"That's where you're wrong, Luce. You may think you've changed a lot, but at your core, you're still the same woman I fell in love with all those years ago. I have seen more strength from you in the last week than most people have in their pinkies. When your mom got hurt, you immediately put your life on hold to care for her. You rearranged the whole house to accommodate her needs, and now you're running her business so it doesn't go under."

"Anybody would have done that for family," she countered, further proving my point. She was stubborn, and if there was one person who wouldn't give up on this, it was her.

"I can promise you that not everybody would have done that. Plus, I'll be with you

every step of the way. You're not alone. We'll figure this out together, okay? And you can always ask your mom for help. I know you don't want to, but she's there to help guide you, sweetheart."

My words seemed to calm her down. Or, at least, so I hoped. "Thank you," she responded once my words got through to her.

"Nothing to thank me for. But, if you do want to thank me." I reached for the bag again, handing her the sandwich I got her. "Eat. You'll need all the strength you can get to tackling this…together."

# Chapter 24

## Lucy

IF THERE WAS one thing that came in handy in all of this, it was that everyone in the town loved my mom. More importantly, everyone had heard of her accident, so they met her misfortune with grace and kindness.

Again, it wasn't something that I was used to in the city, so it was refreshing to experience it in Port-Cartier. It gave me the time I needed to readjust my mom's system.

"Mom, the sticky notes have to go. I'm sorry," I told her the next morning before I was supposed to head to the shop again. Luke and I spent the entire day—and a good portion of last night—sorting through her sticky notes. It wasn't just the orders; it was also her stock, her financial records, and everything in between. I had no idea how she managed to function like this for so long, but the lack of digitalization put her at risk. If something happened to her shop, she would've lost everything she worked so hard to build.

"I like my notes very much, thank you," she retorted, crossing her hands over her chest. She had woken up cranky because Ed wasn't letting her overdue it with walking yesterday, and clearly, her mood was reflected in our conversation, too.

"I know you do, Mom. But it's not good for your business. If you spilled something over your notes, or, if God forbid, something worse happened, you'd lose everything. So, I'm taking it upon myself to handle everything. I'm implementing changes to help you run your business better and quicker. I've already sent a few inquiries about different software. And don't worry, they still come out with printable sheets if you insist on writing everything down, but all of this needs to be deposited somewhere." She'd lose a little bit of money this week, but it'd be better for her in the long run. After yesterday's panic attack, I got to thinking about everything that needed to be done. I decided to take it upon myself to send out the most crucial orders—the wedding bouquets she needed to get done this week, while the flower shops outside our town would handle the smaller orders. It turned out that she wasn't just beloved in Port-Cartier but also the surrounding towns. A week would be enough to start the software I sent inquiries about and add in the pre-existing data. Luke and Mom would both help out with that. It was a good plan; I just needed to get her on board.

"I've run my business for the past twenty years, Luce. And I've been doing it well. All these changes are unnecessary."

I sighed, finally sitting down on the bed beside her. "I know you think so, Mom. I completely understand it. But think about how much time it takes you to write everything down. You could get those things done in just a few clicks when you have software...and then you could give more time to things that *actually* deserve your attention. Like your customers. Or your arrangements." *That* had always been her biggest passion. Not sticky notes.

She crossed her arms over her chest. My mom still didn't look convinced, but if there was one thing I knew that might convince her, it was being able to work even when she was not physically there. We had been on our own for decades before Ed came into the picture, so she was used to working hard and being the breadwinner.

"I don't know, Luce. I don't like changes…"

"Well, how about this? When I introduce the software, I'll get you a second-hand laptop you can use." The one she had at the flower shop was on its last leg. "Then, I'll bring over the laptop to you, and you'll be able to help me as I work at the flower shop. I need all the help I can get, and I…" I trailed off as her face perked up, and I already knew she was convinced. My mom slapped her hands together.

"You know what…maybe you are right. Maybe it *is* time for a change. I mean, I can't just sit here and do nothing. I'll be home-bound for weeks, so if this will allow me to help you out a little…let's do it. And if it doesn't work out, I can always return to my sticky notes." A small laugh escaped my lips as I shook my head.

"I don't think you'll be going back once you see how simple the new system is going to be," I told her. "I'm also going to get you a POS system so you can function like all the other businesses in the twenty-first century."

"I know I'm not overly fond of changes, but I appreciate all the hard work you're putting in, pumpkin. I'm sorry I can't be there to help you with any of this. But Luke seems dedicated to helping you…" Now, there was something else that sparked in her eyes. Curiosity. I already figured out what she wanted to talk about, but it didn't make saying it out loud any simpler.

"He *is* helping you with this new system, isn't he? That's why you're spending so much time together, right?" she asked, trying to make it sound innocent, but I knew she was trying to figure out what was happening with us. The truth was, after we slept together, things got more complicated. I didn't plan for it to happen, but I also couldn't help the feel-ings resurfacing once more. Perhaps they had never left in the first place at all. I'd be lying if I said I didn't think of him over the years more times than I cared to admit.

"He is. He's been a great help," I told her. "And before you ask…I'm not entirely sure what's happening between us. I'm trying to figure it out as I go. I'd just like to leave it at that for now…"

*"Can we talk?" Luke asked, pulling me away from the crowd of people. Things have been good. We still needed to sort out some things after graduating high school, but I was looking forward to college life with him by my side. It felt like a new beginning—one where many more important things would happen. In a few years, we'd buy that house we'd been eyeing for a long time, get married, and have a few kids. Everything was going the way it was meant to. And I was content with it all. I liked the simplicity and the security of it.*

*"Of course." I smiled as I followed him to the base of the giant oak tree we always sat under during our study sessions. When my gaze landed on his face, my stomach turned into knots. Something was wrong. Very wrong.*

*"Luke? Is everything okay?" I asked. "You're so pale—did something happen?" I reached for his hand, but he pulled back. Dread washed over me right away, panic rising right to my throat. The last time he looked like this was when he had to put down his dog. His family no longer had a dog, so….*

*"I don't know how to do this," Luke began, looking away from me.*

*"Just say it," I quickly told him. "Did something happen? Did someone—"*

*"No, no, it's nothing like that," he assured me. When his eyes returned to mine, they were filled with tears. "Luce, I think we should break up."*

*A small, involuntary laugh escaped my lips. The reaction didn't make sense, but it was the one my body had given me—mostly because I didn't believe it was real. It had to be a prank he was playing on me. There was no way he just said we should break up.*

*"Stop. It's not funny."*

*"I'm not joking. I think it may be for the best."*

*My heart dropped at his words. There was no way this was happening—we were just about to begin a new chapter of our lives together. We had our entire life planned out. Everyone knew it. And everyone admired how mature and secure we were together.*

*"You...seriously want to break up?" I repeated, hoping that was some sick joke. My brain couldn't comprehend what he was saying. It made zero sense. He loved me, I knew he did.*

*"We're about to go to college. We're about to leave this town. I just...I think we should experience everything the world has to offer. We've been together for so long, and I don't want either of us to miss out—"*

*"What?" I asked again because this couldn't be happening. My body hit me with many different physiological reactions, but none were positive. The most prominent was ringing in my ears that I could barely handle.*

*"I've just given it a lot of thought lately. And I'm not sure about our plan anymore..."*

*My eyes welled up, and I felt sick. In fact, I was pretty sure I was about to throw up at any point now. Maybe all over him. I reared back like I'd been hit. My whole body shook, desperate to get away from him.*

*"I'm sorry, Lu—"*

*"Don't you dare!" I yelled at him. I didn't want to hear any excuses after he strung me along. A few people looked at us, but it was the last thing I cared about. "And take your fucking promise ring." I struggled to get it off my finger, almost dislocating my finger in the process. As I hurled the ring in his direction, it hit him right in the face.*

*Good, he deserved it.*

*More tears flooded my eyes as I turned on my heels and ran, desperate never to see him again.*

That was the last time I saw him—before returning this year. After that, my life took a very different turn. I dropped out of the college that I was going to attend across the river from Luke's college. Instead, I got accepted to a community college in California. My mom wasn't too happy about me being so far away from home, but she knew I needed to get away from Port-Cartier if I wanted to keep any last shreds of my sanity. She helped me pack up my car and drive to California, and I never looked back.

Until now.

Luke claimed he was different now, and I wanted to believe him. But ten years ago, he broke my heart out of the blue. How could I be sure it wouldn't happen again?

# Chapter 25
## Lucy

MY MOM'S blessing made implementing changes in the flower shop much easier. It was going quicker, too. Or so it felt, at least. I barely noticed it was night since I spent most of the day fiddling with the new POS system I had ordered for her. I wanted to put everything in place as quickly as possible to ensure she didn't change her mind.

When the door opened, I realized I was only halfway through the manual. The other shops had long closed, leaving our shop the only place with lights on in the tiny street where my mom's flower shop was located.

Over the past few days, Luke had been assisting me at the flower shop. I greatly appreciated his help, but I insisted he took care of his business today, since he had a customer coming over. He left sometime during midday to get a few things done at his shop and tend to the customer who had stopped by. I didn't expect him to be back today.

Yet, there he was—right in the middle of the flower shop, with a slight smile on his lips.

If one were to ask him, he would've gladly ditched *all* of his work to be by my side. As much as I appreciated it, I couldn't ask him to abandon his job for the sake of my mother's. He tried to convince me it would be fine, but work piled up quickly, and I didn't want him to regret it later.

"What brings you here?" I asked before a smile spread over my face.

"You didn't answer your phone, so I thought I would check here first to see if you're still alive."

"Oh, sorry, I've been knee-deep in sorting out all these sticky notes and the POS system, so I didn't realize you called." I quickly rummaged through the endless papers to find my phone and three missed calls from him and two from my mom.

As my gaze rose again, the vision of him there flooded my stomach with a sudden wave of nostalgia.

*"Mom? I'm done with school," I called, looking around as I stepped into the flower shop. She was nowhere to be found, and the lights were dimmed, too. With a sigh, I closed the door behind me. Mom wasn't at the front counter, which usually meant she was in the back making bouquets—but even then, she always responded when I called out for her. I stepped further into the shop.*

*Luke had baseball practice after school, so I grabbed a ride with Rachel. I hoped I'd see him soon. With the prom and graduation coming up, there were things we needed to figure out.*

*"Mom?" I called again. As I stepped into the back room, instead of my mom, I found Luke. He stood there, surrounded by a sea of flowers. My eyes practically popped out of my head at the sight—I knew he likely asked for my mom's help, but still. How was he able to get his hands on so many flowers? In his hands was a bouquet of peonies and baby breath—my favorite. I blinked frantically, trying to chase the tears away. I could feel them coming.*

*There was so much to take in that I nearly missed the sign before him that read, 'Roses are red, violets are blue, PROM would be amazing with you.'*

*"What are you doing here?" I asked, even if it was…more than obvious. Luke had always been kind and mindful, surprising me with gestures that every girl dreamed of. Acts of service had always*

*been one of his main love languages, but this was a lot—even for him.*

*Luke didn't answer. Instead, he asked, "Will you go to prom with me?" I squealed and leaped into his arms. He quickly caught me, and I pressed my lips against his. My heart thudded inside my chest so fast it felt like it might burst with happiness.*

*"Of course, I'll go to prom with you. What kind of a question is that?" There wasn't anyone I'd even dream of going with but him. "Though all of this is slightly cheesy, I've got to admit."*

*Luke chuckled, kissing me once more. "I needed to bring my A-game to impress my girl."*

*"And you've managed," I told him. Slowly, he put me back down as my mom came out with tears in her eyes. I already suspected she had something to do with this, too.*

*"You two are so cute."*

"Luce?" Luke called out, luring me back into the present. This town had been so full of memories that they flooded me when I least expected them. Back in Seattle, I could avoid them, but here they were inevitable. Especially in the presence of my first—and only—true love.

"Sorry," I said as I blinked once. "I just...got distracted. What were you saying?"

"I thought I'd take you to dinner since I figured you hadn't eaten lunch," he pointed out, slinging his hands into his pockets. Now, it wasn't the thoughts of the distant past that flooded me, but the memory of what we did here only days ago. His body against mine and— "So, what do you say?"

I smiled. "It's like you know me or something."

"Or something," Luke repeated with a small smile. I knew we should talk about what happened, but I wasn't sure I was ready yet. "I've already taken the liberty of making a reservation."

"How do you know what I like to eat now? It's been ten years since you were last familiar with my taste..." I trailed off. Luke closed the space between us in a few short steps. Once he stood before me, his scent hit my nostrils, intoxicating me immediately. I stalled in my movement as he towered over me, his fingers reaching for a stray strand of my hair. The movement was innocent, but it was enough to send a wave of goosebumps down my skin anyway.

"I am familiar with the taste of you *again*," he murmured, his eyes locked on mine. The intensity of his gaze made me want to look away, as did the suggestive tone of his voice, but I resisted the urge to do so. "But regarding your question…I believe your love for pasta has remained timeless, so I'm taking you to the place with the best pasta in Port-Cartier." The smile on his lips would've been enough to make me agree to anything he asked of me right then.

"Are you asking me out on a date, Luke?" His lips were a breath away from mine. Half of me expected him to lean down and kiss me, but he didn't. The tension rose higher, to the point where I suspected it was only a matter of time before we lost ourselves in it.

"Yes, I suppose I am. So, what do you say, Luce?"

The fluttering sensation in my stomach grew more prominent. I had feared opening myself to something like this for so long. What I had with Luke didn't compare with anything I experienced with any man after him. It was all surface-level, but I convinced myself I was happy with it.

Now, the kind of intimacy and connection I craved all along was staring at me again. A part of me was hesitant to let him back in. Having my heart broken by him again would destroy me. I was sure of it. This time, now even running away from this town wouldn't save me like it did the last time.

Yet, the softness of his gaze was all-consuming.

"I say yes," I responded and grabbed my purse, realizing I had been silent too long. "And I have high expectations about this pasta place of yours."

Al Dente, the restaurant Luke took me to, was newly opened in Port-Cartier and near the beach. The terrace overlooked the sea, each wave gently lulling toward us while the city lights twinkled in the water's reflection. While most of the town's restaurants and cafes boasted a bohemian, coastal vibe, Al Dente embraced a more rustic charm. The restaurant was different from any other in the area with its exposed brick walls, lush greenery, and wooden terrace.

Our table was near the fence, giving us much-needed privacy as we sat down. I thought I should have gone home and dressed up for the occasion, but Luke didn't let me go another minute without getting something to eat.

"Stop it," he said. "I can already tell what you're thinking."

I pressed my lips into a thin line, arcing my brow. "There's no way you can tell what I'm thinking." It was a thing back in the day—he could practically read my mind, but how likely was he still able to do it after all these years?

"You're thinking about how much you wish you had changed before coming here...and I'm here to tell you that you're the most beautiful woman in Port-Cartier, Luce."

A smile threatened to cross my face, but I held it back. Luke always had a way of sweet-talking his way into my heart. "You're a little biased."

"I just have eyes..."

"Welcome to Al Dente," the tall waitress chirped as she approached our table, handing us each the menu. The words were mainly directed at me, though, as I suspected that Luke had come here before. "I'm Nora, and I'll be your waitress for the night."

"It's good to see you, Nora. I see the business is going well tonight," Luke retorted, and he was right. The place was packed with people tonight, to the point where I wondered how he managed to get us a table here in the first place on such short notice.

"It's a busy night," Nora confirmed. "But never too busy for you. We *had* to squeeze you in with a table for two." I lifted my brow slightly, unsure if she was just overly enthusiastic over the fact Luke was here as a regular or if she was hitting on him. Either way, Luke's attention turned toward me.

"You should try their carbonara."

I opened the menu. Al Dente had a wide selection of different kinds of Italian pasta, but he still remembered my favorite. "It's really good. It's my favorite meal here."

"Then a carbonara it is." I shut the menu, not bothering to look at anything else.

"For me, as well," Luke told Nora, who then took the menus. After we ordered our drinks—a glass of wine for me and some water for him—she was gone. "I don't drink when I drive," he explained when I met his beverage choice with a question in my eyes.

"Fair enough. By the way, I didn't know you were also a fan of carbonara." When we were together, he'd tease me about how often my mom made that meal for me. Like many other things, I had left that love behind long after leaving Port-Cartier.

"I wasn't. This restaurant opened when I first got back to Port-Cartier. And when I first came here…it was the meal listed at the top. It made me think of you, so I decided to try it out. And I've been a fan ever since." My heart clutched at his words, but it didn't seem he was done yet. "Luce"—he reached for my hand, his gaze soft—"I know this can't be easy for you. I messed up in the past. I broke your heart. And you have no reason to believe me. I know that, too. But I have spent the past decade thinking about you. Nothing I ever tried to share with anyone else could compare to what we had. I realized I had made a mistake a long time ago by letting you go…and I wasn't brave enough to fix it. I am now. I want you back. I want to spend the rest of my days with you. It's a big ask—I know, but we have to start from somewhere. And I suggest we start from right here. Right now."

"Luke…" I practically choked out the word. There were dozens of people around us, yet each word he said carried so much weight that the rest of the world didn't even exist. It was just the two of us.

"I know life is complicated now, and that's entirely my fault. I let it get complicated. You have the life you've built in Seattle, and mine is here…but if you give me a chance, I know we can make it work. I'll make sure not a day goes by without me counting the biggest blessing I have in my life—you. It's *always* been you. And I know I have no right to ask for another chance…but I'm begging for one, anyway." When I didn't respond, he quickly continued, "I know you feel it, too. But if by some chance you don't…tell me, and we never have to speak about this again."

I only then realized that our hands had been interlocked this entire time. He was right. So many things remained unsolved, and so many obstacles would be in front of us if we decided to do this…but I felt it as much as he did.

"I don't know how this would work," I admitted. Nora gave us a much-needed break as she brought our drinks over, placing my glass of wine in front of me. I took a big sip of the much-needed liquid courage. "As you said, we have built our lives in two entirely different places…"

Luke nodded. I knew this would be hard, yet I couldn't deny that being without him would be even harder. In fact, I wasn't even sure I wanted to do it in the first place. How could things ever be the same again after this?

"How about this. You're going to stay here for the summer. So, maybe we can give this a proper shot while you're here. And, if by the end of it, you're sure you want to do this, we'll find a way to make it happen." With the hopeful look that twinkled in his eyes, it was difficult to even think about saying no to his request.

"I can't promise anything…" I told him sincerely. Sure, all of this sounded nice now, but it would be time for action instead of words at the end of the summer. And moving life from one location to another wasn't as simple as he made it sound. I'd know. I left my life once, and it was one of the hardest things I had ever done.

When Nora brought our pasta to us, I had forgotten all about food. My focus shifted to one thing and one thing only: the question that left his lips, which would be the turning point of my life all over again.

"Are you willing to give this a shot? 'Cause I'm all in, Luce. It's you and me against the world."

My heart already knew the answer. All that was left to do was to say it out loud.

"Yes," I said softly, "I'm willing to give it a shot."

# Chapter 26
## Luke

"I HAVE SOME NEWS, but I do *not* want you to freak out, and I do *not* want you to make a big deal out of it," I told my mom as I visited my childhood home during the obligatory family Sunday lunches. Landon and I had moved out, and Logan was in the process of doing so, but Mom insisted that we all meet every Sunday to have lunch together. Especially during summertime when it was BBQ season—my family's favorite.

I stared out the window at the massive oak tree that provided much-needed shade. Beneath it, my father and two brothers were already setting up the BBQ. My mom kept her eyes on the potatoes. She and I were on potato duty today, while the rest of the family was already out and setting up the BBQ.

"What is it?" she asked. "If you're about to ask me to make bread for you again—"

A small laugh left my lips. That was a fair assumption— she made the best bread, and though she'd pretend to be annoyed whenever I'd ask her to make me a loaf, I knew deep down that she enjoyed the compliment. "It's not that, mom. It's about Lucy."

Instantly, she put down the peeler, turning toward me. Her expression radiated impatience, though she tried not to push.

"I'm listening," she said softly, with her hand on her hip.

"Well, I didn't want to tell this to anyone yet, but you are my mother, so...two nights ago, I asked Luce to give us another chance." Her eyes widened. I could recall just how heartbroken she was when the two of us broke up. Luce had always been the daughter she never had but always wanted. And I took that away from her with my foolish actions. It was also partially why she was the first person I wanted to share the news with. I wanted to, somehow and to some extent, lessen the damage I made all those years ago. Not only to Luce but to everyone around us. "And she said yes. We're not official—I didn't want to strain her like that yet, but we are exclusive, I suppose, and we're taking things slow to see where they lead us."

My mom made a feeble attempt to hide an excited squeal, but she failed as she threw her arms around me, wrapping me into a tight hug.

"Oh, Luke. I'm so happy for you. I knew the two of you were eventually going to find your way back to each other...I didn't expect it to take a decade." She squeezed me tightly. I gave her a small pat on the back to prompt her to pull back. We had potatoes to get back to. "But that doesn't matter. You're back together now, and you have the rest of your lives to compensate for the time you spent away from each other."

"Mom, it's not like that," I admitted. Clearly, none of my words got through to her aside from the ones she *wanted* to hear. The truth was, I still wasn't sure how all of this would work. Luce had a life she built in Seattle, and it felt wrong to ask her to leave it behind and come back here, even if there was a school here that would benefit greatly from her skill set. And I had taken over my father's business a little while ago. I couldn't just leave it just when I started implementing internal changes. It was my father's life work; he entrusted me with it, and I wanted to make sure it was taken care of. Still, figuring all of it out seemed much less complicated than the thought of losing Luce again. "We still have a lot to figure out, but as I said, we're willing to give it a proper shot while she's here…"

Behind me, Landon cleared his throat. I turned back to find him standing at the wooden frame that connected the kitchen and the back porch.

"We'll talk about this later," my mom told me, giving me a small pat on the shoulder. I had no doubt she couldn't wait to share the news with my dad, but at least she tried to be discreet in front of my brother. At least until she leaned in closer to me, *trying* to whisper, but she was far too excited for it actually to be silent. "Maybe she could join us for the BBQ next week."

I wasn't sure if we were quite there yet with our relationship, but Landon came to my rescue before we could discuss it any further. "Why don't you come to help me get the beers from the garage?"

I nodded, following along to get away from my *very* enthusiastic mother. I thought I was safe from discussing my new relationship the moment I stepped out on the porch and headed toward the garage, but Landon proved me wrong.

"So…you and Luce, huh?" he asked, turning toward me as we entered the garage. It was a space where our dad accumulated his never-ending list of projects around the house. Now that he was retired, he had a lot of time on his hands.

"You heard that?" I slung my hands into my pockets. It wasn't too often that Landon could join us for lunch—if you ask my mom—because of his busy schedule, but when he did join us, he was usually overly observant. Like today.

"I did. I'm happy for you. I really am. I like her."

"I'm sensing there's a but coming…" I let out a small laugh. Landon was older than me, and with that came an entirely different perspective on life. One that I often couldn't see with my own two eyes.

"But you've both built separate lives. Surely you know that. And if you want this to work, you may have to be willing to make certain sacrifices. I know you didn't stop loving her as you claimed all those years ago when you broke up with her, but that will be a continuous thought in the back of her mind."

His words stung, but they carried the truth I couldn't deny. I ran my fingers through my hair, letting what he just said marinate in his mind. If she could only see how much love I held for her in my heart, there would never be a single doubt about the sincerity of my intentions ever again. Sadly, the world didn't function that way, and I could only rely on my words and actions to transfer my feelings into reality.

"I know. I fucked up—massively. I want to do my best to make things right. She deserves it."

Landon retrieved a six-pack of beers from the garage fridge. We often joked that it was our dad's secret stash, but he was happy to share it with us every Sunday when we came over.

"I know you're not asking for my advice—"

I smiled. "But you're going to give it to me anyway."

"That's what big brothers are for," Landon retorted. We didn't get to spend as much time together as we'd like because of work, but the time we did get together was always valuable. "Don't move too fast, Luke. I know you're eager to make things right and prove to her how much you love her… but she's going to need time. And you need to be selfless enough to give it to her."

It was a strange concept, really. We'd spend a decade away from each other—it felt like spending another second away from each other's presence was the last thing we should want to do, but it made sense.

"I thought you were a doctor," I told him. "Not a certified

relationship expert. But I guess you're a two-in-one kind of a man like you've always been."

Landon laughed. "Well, I am older than you. I know a thing or two. And with how excited Mom got, I figured she wasn't about to be the one to tell you any of this."

"Come on, you two," Mom called out from the front porch. "There's no way getting beer takes this long to retrieve them. The potatoes aren't going to peel themselves, and Landon, your father needs help with starting the BBQ."

Landon's brow shot up, and he slapped his palms together. "Well, you've heard her. Time to move. Just try to keep in mind what I've told you." The firmness of his tone made me wonder if there was something he wasn't telling me —if he was sharing this advice from his own experience. While my family was close by all means, there were still aspects of our lives that we liked to keep private. Landon especially.

When I returned to the kitchen, my mom still had that excited expression. "Just so you know, I meant it. We'd love to have Luce for lunch next Sunday." I did, too. In fact, I hoped that someday we'd have a tradition like that of our own.

# Chapter 27
## *Lucy*

"YOU KNOW, I think this isn't working out. Sticky notes may be the best organizational tool I've ever had," my mom grumbled over the phone. Being stuck at the house made her more grumpy than usual. She was used to moving around, used to running her own business. Putting all her trust into someone else's hands—even if they were her daughter's—must have been hard. Still, I expected at least *some* cooperation, and she gave me practically none.

"You say that now, but wait until it's all fully set up. You'll love it, Mom. I promise," I assured her. Granted, right now, she was stuck with the more tedious part of the work, which was inputting years' worth of information into the second-hand laptop I got for her. She was, as she put it, *a certified technology hater*, but I hoped she'd soon see it wasn't all that bad. "I wish I were there to help you, but someone's got to get the actual orders out."

I stepped back, eyeing the bouquet of red roses and baby's breath I'd put together for one of the customers. It came with an 'I'm sorry' note, so I hoped its richness would send the message along. The person who ordered it was also unknown to me, so I guessed it was a tourist passing by, which made me much more nervous. Most of the time, my mom was familiar with her client's tastes—all of them were return customers.

She continued babbling over the phone, "I don't understand why I can't come to help. I'd sit next to you and instruct you with creating—"

"You can't come over and help because the doctor told you so. You have a long road to recovery ahead of you, Mom. We don't want it to be any longer than it has to be, do we?" On the other side of the line, she sighed. "Look, I know this is hard for you. But I spent all of my high school years here with you, and I need you to trust me that I remember a thing or two."

"I trust you, pumpkin," my mom responded. Now, there was a little bit of defeat in her tone. "I just don't like being away from my store. You and that store are my life, you know."

I smiled, even if a slight burn was present behind my eyes. She risked everything—both to open up this store and to raise me as a single mom who worked hard. I wanted this to be my way of paying back a fraction of everything she's done for me.

The bell over the door rang, dragging my attention away from our phone call. "I know, Mom. And I promise I'm doing my best to implement the changes that are going to help you run this place smoother than ever."

My mom sighed. "Well, I suppose I do see how it will be simpler once all the hard work is done..." As she hangs up, I approach an elderly woman in a bright orange tracksuit. It was impossible to mistake her for anyone else, even after a decade had passed since the last time I saw her.

"Mrs. Fairmont! How are you?" I asked, straightening the apron with all my tools. A smile spread over my lips. Mrs. Fairmont was a part of many of my favorite high school memories.

"Lucy! I heard you were back. I can't believe it." She smiled in return. "Tell me, how's my favorite student?"

"I'm good," I laughed as she approached me. She didn't care about the messy apron, nor did she care that we hadn't seen each other in ten years as she pulled me into a hug. I returned it. "Although, I'm sure you've had other favorite students since you taught me in high school."

"Pssh," Mrs. Fairmont countered. "Haven't you heard? I'm teaching in elementary school now. We have a shortage of teachers here, so I transferred to help out." When she stepped back, her hand remained in my arms as she took a good look at me. "I'm glad you're back. God knows your mother is happy. Especially now that she's home bound. And I've never seen that boy Luke happier. He's been lonely that one." My stomach did a flop at that. With our decision to start seeing each other again happening so suddenly, we still didn't discuss many aspects. I supposed that our past was meant to stay in the past, but I couldn't deny that some curiosity sparked in me.

"I know he was your second favorite student, Mrs. Fairmont, but you don't need to put in a good word...He's already earned my fondness."

Mrs. Fairmont shook her head. "Oh, no, I'm not trying to do that. I mean it—he's been lonely ever since you two broke up. We all noticed it."

"You haven't seen...Luke with anyone after we broke up?" I pried, not sure if I wanted to know the answer. I supposed it didn't make a difference, but he did mention a masseuse girlfriend once. Was he just messing around when he said it?

"No, you both left, and he returned a few years later. He bought that house you two had always admired and has been fixing it up for years now...I think he always hoped that you would come back. If you ask anyone else in the town, I think they'll tell you the same." My mom and I had an unspoken agreement—ever since I left the town, Luke was one topic we wouldn't bring up under any circumstances. I didn't want to hear anything about him after I left because I thought it was much easier for him than for me. "Are you planning to stay here?"

"Oh, I'm not sure," I quickly said. All of this was overwhelming. While I agreed to start dating Luke again, we hadn't thought everything through, and I was suddenly hyper-aware of it. "I was planning to stay here for as long as I can to help my mom…"

"Well, if you do decide to stay, we need more teachers in our elementary school, and we'd be delighted to have you. The offer is there, but don't feel pressured," Mrs. Fairmont told me, collecting the bouquet she had ordered before leaving. I didn't want to think about anything I had just learned, so I busied myself making bouquets for an upcoming wedding.

If there was one thing Mom was right about, it was that it was easy to get lost in her kind of work. It really brought the creative side out of me, too. One I had long forgotten but truly enjoyed.

The door rang once more sometime after Mrs. Fairmont had left. This time, my heart skipped a little as it set on Luke. He wore a simple white T-shirt with black jeans, yet he looked as effortlessly dashing as always.

"Hey," he said as he approached me, leaning down and pressing a soft kiss against my lips. After agreeing to date him again, I supposed this was my new reality, but it wasn't any less unfamiliar. More flutters spread through my stomach, and though I had long forgotten them, I liked the feeling.

"Hey," I replied softly. Luke brushed a disobedient curl out of my face before placing a mint lemonade on my desk. He had me so taken aback that I hadn't even noticed he came in bearing presents. "And thank you."

"You're welcome, sweetheart. I figured you could use the

refreshment. I stopped by your mom's today to bring over a pie my mom had made, and Eve told me you had been stuck here the entire day."

I chuckled. "Did she also complain about being stuck inputting information into the software?"

Amusement sparked on his face as he nodded. "Of course. In fact, she spent a good fifteen minutes complaining just about that." I took a sip of my lemonade. It was quickly growing on me, likely on the way to becoming my favorite beverage. I lifted the cup, offering some to him, but Luke shook his head. "No, that's for you. While I wanted you to have it, I also came in with an ulterior motive…"

"We are *not* having sex in here again," I quickly told him, though I wasn't *entirely* opposed to the idea. Luke rounded the counter and stood behind me, his hands on my back again. I closed my eyes, enjoying the firmness of his touch as he worked through the knots spread across my behind. Momentarily, I wondered if he did date someone who taught him to massage like this, but the words remained unspoken.

"With how loud and wet you were the last time, I don't think it would take much to convince you to let me be inside you here again, but luckily for you…" Luke leaned in, pressing a soft kiss to my neck. I shuddered. *Damn him.* He was right. "I'm not here to have sex with you. Although, I wouldn't say no. Instead, I'm here to ask if you could join me for a family BBQ next Sunday. No pressure, though."

I knew him well enough to know how all of this played out, even after all these years. "You've told your mom, haven't you?"

Luke's laughter filled the air, its sincerity making the rest of the world fade into insignificance. It was both exhilarating and terrifying. I had only been here for a short while, and all my defenses were already crumbling. I had promised myself to be cautious, but I could barely think at that moment, let alone guard my heart.

"I couldn't help it. I'm the happiest I've been in a long time, and she would've asked about a million questions in front of everyone..." His touch grew firmer, hitting all the right spots. I tipped my head back, closing my eyes. I didn't have anything against the BBQs at their home. In fact, they were some of the more prominent memories from our relationship. Always filled with laughter, always so fun.

"I see. And you don't think this is a little too soon?" I questioned.

Luke's fingers stalled on my back momentarily. "If you think it is, we don't have to—"

"Of course, I'd love to come. Your parents and Logan helped me set everything up for my mom when she fell, so how can I say no?" Opening my eyes, I looked back at him. He was already staring at me adoringly. "Though...I do have one request," I murmured.

"Anything you'd like..."

"There's karaoke night next week and—"

Luke's loud groan interrupted my sentence. Granted, I wasn't a big fan of the karaoke, nor was I a good singer, but Luke hated them, which made them so damn fun. It was an actual test of this new relationship of ours. I batted my lashes at him.

"Are you seriously going to say no to me?"

He sighed, but I didn't miss the teasing glint in his eyes. "I could never say no to you. So, yes, sure, we'll do the karaoke night."

# Chapter 28
## *Lucy*

THE FOLLOWING DAY, the red rose and baby breath bouquet remained unpicked. I stared at it, along with the phone number attached to the order. Things like this happened sometimes—sometimes customers forgot they had ordered flowers or mistakenly didn't set up a delivery.

And my mom always made it her mission to notify them about it, so it was up to me to do the same. With a small sigh, I grabbed my phone and dialed the number. The name linked to the order was Jensen Powell, repeating in my head repeatedly as the phone rang. The person on the other side finally picked up at the fifth ring.

"Mr. Powell, my name is Lucy, and I'm calling from Blushing Blooms about your flower order. You haven't set up a delivery, and the bouquet was meant to be picked up three hours ago, so I'm just calling to check if there's anything we can do. Has there been some mistake on our end?"

"No," a voice, unmistakably familiar, said over the phone. "There hasn't been a mistake. The order is exactly where it's meant to be."

*Jason.*

*What the hell?*

"What in the world are you doing, Jason? You're not Jensen Powell, and I surely don't have the time for your nonsense. Did you put in a fake order or something?"

"No, Luce, the order is real. I wanted you to get the flowers and the apology note I attached to it. Have you read it?"

"I haven't. I printed it out and attached it to the flowers, and that was about as interested I was in anything Jensen—or you—have to say."

"Read the note, Luce. Please. I know…" Jason choked on his words on the other side of the line. I should have felt something—after all, he was my last relationship and one I was running from this time. At the very least, I thought I would be seeking closure. But I was surprised to realize I didn't care about any of it. At all. And it was the most liberating feeling in the world. "I know I messed up, and I know you don't owe me anything, but I just wanted you to know that I see now that I've made such a massive mistake, and I couldn't be more sorry about it. So, I figured that if I sent you flowers—"

"You didn't *send* me flowers. I had to make the bouquet myself. And then call you to check if there was a mistake on my end with the delivery. It's hardly romantic." Wheels started turning in my head. "Wait, how did you even know I'd be here?"

"It doesn't matter. I figured it out because I want to be with you again, and I wanted you to see the lengths I'd go to win you over again. I don't know who that—"

"So, that's what all of this is about. You're threatened by the other guy you've heard from me the other day, aren't you? That's the only reason you're calling. You can't accept the fact that someone else has something *you* lost. You don't care about me, nor do you want me back. You just don't want anyone else to have me. That's all." I let out a small snort.

Weeks ago, I would've been upset about all of this, but it was entertaining right now. While some things changed and grew, some did not. Some were always doomed to stay the same and ruin your life; my relationship with Jason was at the top of that list.

"Please, just hear me out—"

"I'm going to say this one time, and one time only. Even if I weren't seeing someone else, I wouldn't ever consider getting back with you. You betrayed my trust in the worst way possible, and frankly, you treated me like shit for the rest of our relationship, too. I see that now, and I don't ever want you to call me again."

I didn't waste another second on him as I hung up.

*What an asshole,* I thought to myself. The audacity he had never failed to amaze me. If there was one good thing to come out of that conversation, though, it was the realization that I hadn't called Sailor and needed to check up on my best friend, too. With my hectic life, I barely had the time to breathe, but I wanted to keep her updated on everything.

ME: Are you free to call?

Sailor didn't bother responding; instead, my phone rang right away. I picked up with a small smile on my face. It was hard to believe I felt *good* after what should have been a difficult conversation with an ex-boyfriend.

My best friend sighed. "I see you only now remember the life you've left behind."

"I know, I'm sorry. I didn't mean to. I'm practically modernizing my mom's flower shop, and it's taking up a lot of my time. But that's not all. I also…"

"Found some hot guy you've been spending all your time with? That's the only acceptable end of that sentence, Luce."

I couldn't help the small laugh that filled the room. I found myself pacing around, nervous to say the words out loud. Sometimes, they still didn't feel real in the first place—perhaps that was partially the issue.

"Well, I suppose that's right...to some extent."

"Oh. My. God. It's Luke, isn't it? You two got back together, haven't you? Girl, I need to hear everything! Spare no detail. Oh, God. I will have to fly down to you to meet him officially and give him a piece of my mind. If he hurts you again..." She trailed off. The smile on my face widened. I truly appreciated her enthusiasm. It meant more than she'd ever know.

"It is Luke. But we're taking things slow and trying to see where it will take us..."

"Okay..." Sailor dragged the word out as if more things were on her mind. "Well, did you discuss how all of it will work? I mean, if things are great, I'm guessing he's going to come to Seattle with you and—"

"It's not that simple. He took over his dad's company when his dad retired. So, he has a lot to do around here," I explained, nervously fidgeting with the edge of my apron. Now that I was saying it aloud, I saw how ridiculous we were not discussing that aspect of our lives. It was a one-way ticket to more pain that neither of us wanted to experience.

"I see," Sailor responded, though some uncertainty still laced her tone. "Well, as long as you know what you're doing, you know I support you, girl. I just don't want you to get hurt. But with that said...I just need to know if you've already done the deed."

"Sailor..."

"Oh my God! You did it! You did it, and you didn't call me to let me know!" she screeched on the other side of the line, though it was all in a teasing tone. "Seriously, Luce, what kind of a friend are you if you're not letting me live vicariously through you? Tell me everything!"

My cheek reddened, burning from her question. "It was fantastic. He's…amazing. I didn't even know orgasms like that were possible. That's all the information I'm giving you for now."

"Ah, thank you. That's all I needed to know—that you're well taken care of. I, unfortunately, have an admission of my own, Luce." Her tone now grew more serious. I froze at it. It wasn't often that Sailor spoke in that tone, so it must have been something bad.

"What is it? Is everything okay? Are you—"

"Everything's okay, Luce. I…I went to get your things a little while ago. I wanted to call you to tell you all about it, but I was embarrassed, I guess. With how I handled all of it. I got there, and I barely held back the urge to punch Jason in the throat. Seriously, he's quite possibly the worst person ever to exist. Your things were packed, but some of them were missing. And I wasn't about to let that asshole have a single thing of yours that didn't belong to him," Sailor spoke so quickly she barely had the time to breathe. It often happened when she was nervous, which made *me* nervous.

"Sailor, breathe. Whatever happened—it's okay. You've done everything—"

"I fucked up, Lucy. I really did. I lost my temper when I figured out he's purposely keeping some of your things so he'd have the excuse to invite you over when you return to Seattle. Seriously, what kind of a person does that? Anyway, I told him that I'm not letting him keep your shit when you don't know when you're going to come back because your mom is still recovering…and that triggered some shitty plan in his mind to win you over. He broke up with Sarah, apparently. I'm not surprised. I'm shocked anyone wanted to put up with his shit in the first place. Anyway, I'm so sorry…"

"Sailor," I said as my shoulders relaxed. It wasn't nearly as bad as I expected. His plan had come through, and it didn't affect me in the slightest. In fact, it only made me more thankful that I had Luke by my side. "He planned to send me flowers. Actually, he ordered them from my mom's flower shop, so I had to make them myself." I rolled my eyes. "They came with a note I didn't even want to read. No notes and no flowers can make up for what he did. I'm going to toss the note and bring the flowers to one of our elderly neighbors who will love them."

Sailor still sounded unsure over the phone. "So…everything's okay?"

I smiled. "Everything's okay. You don't have anything to worry about. You've done more for me than any other friend I've ever had has. Even if you did do something, I'd never hold it against you. But you didn't. I appreciate everything you've done for me more than you know." A slight sniffle echoed on the other side. My own eyes started welling up, too. "Don't tell me you're crying."

"I'm not. I'm not. I, *uh*, I've just got something in my eye. Nothing to worry about." Silence. "And I miss you. This is the longest we've been apart since we met, you know. And I didn't even get to punch Jason or light him on fire."

Now, both of us laughed. In fact, we laughed until my stomach hurt. Even if I kept myself busy for the most part, I felt the ache, too. I missed her as well. She was the best friend I had ever had, and she stood by me through everything.

"Well, I can't help you with a missed opportunity with Jason, but…whenever you'd like, you're more than welcome to visit. My mom's in the guest room downstairs, so you'd be getting her room for yourself…"

Sailor squealed. "Stop. The queen's room all for me? Sign me up right now." She chuckled. At that moment, we weren't separated by miles of distance. We were beside each other, just like in the good old times. "I need to figure out work, but I may take you up on that offer, you know."

"I hope you will. We'd love to have you here."

Port-Cartier offered a lot for both familiar and first-time visitors, and I was beginning to see that all over again.

# Chapter 29
## Luke

THERE WEREN'T many things I disliked—aside from the ones most people frowned upon—but karaoke had to be at the top of that list. And I already knew it was what made it so appealing to Luce. I leaned against my truck as I waited for her in front of her home, and my mind suddenly flooded with images of the past.

How often had I come here when we were teenagers, waiting for her before our date? Back then, I came to pick her up in my shitty used car that broke down more often than it drove properly. Still, it never let me down for our dates. And surely, at least a few of them were karaoke dates.

I couldn't have said no to her then, and apparently, I couldn't say no to her now, either.

My gaze washed over her as the front door opened and Luce exited. She wore a flowy, knee-length dress. The dark red fabric complimented her skin beautifully, and her hair was let down—just how I liked it. Her curls were one of my favorite features, and it made me happy to see them in all their glory.

As she approached me with that sweet smile of hers, I found it impossible to resist. Leaning down, I pressed my lips against hers, savoring her taste. Her smile bled into our kiss, infecting me, too. When I pulled back, she lightly patted my cheek.

"Ready to sing your heart out?" she asked me, nudging me slightly as I opened the door for her and groaned. I could do many things. I was skilled with my hands, a great cook, and relatively good at skiing, but singing was certainly not my strongest suit.

"You're lucky I lo—" Before I could finish the sentence Landon warned me against, the words stuck to my throat. Luce tensed slightly, too, as if she could sense what I was about to say. "You're lucky you're impossible to say no to. I wouldn't do karaoke with anyone else."

"Mm, Linda said otherwise. From what I heard, you were putting up a show nearly every night when you were younger." A smile threatened to play on my lips as I shut the door for her and settled on the driver's seat. It seemed like my mom was physically incapable of keeping secrets.

"That was the past, Luce. This is present. I'm a changed man," I told her as I started my truck. The karaoke night took place in Rockwood in a bar named Neon Nectar. Ironically enough, I hadn't been there for exactly a decade. Ever since she left. "Speaking of past and present, how's everything going at Blushing Blooms?" I wanted to be there to help out as much as possible, but Luce insisted I had to take care of my own business, too; even if I tried to explain to her that I was able to take a few days off—it would have no impact on my work.

"It's going well. We're finally almost done with inputting all the information from the sticky notes my mom had accumulated. Honestly, I have nightmares about sticky notes. If I see one more…" She shook her head. "I need to write down instructions for her so she knows how to use the system and doesn't get confused. I know her—if she doesn't get it right away, she will want to give up."

My eyes remained on the road before us, but I listened intently to her. Instinctively, my hand drifted from the gearshift to her thigh, resting there.

*How I had missed this,* I thought to myself but decided against saying the words out loud.

"You're doing great. She must be so proud of you. I know I am." A dense forest surrounded us to our left. Given the Port-Cartier coastal position, it was the only place providing the shade we desperately needed during the hot summer months. No matter the heat outside, the forest was always chilly and perfect for a relaxing walk.

But that wasn't all there was to it.

It was also the place Luce and I frequented when we first started dating—usually to make out, but later in our relationship, occasionally to do even more…

I quickly chased away the thoughts—or I tried to, at least, until Luce's voice echoed through my truck.

"Pull up at our spot," she said. Suddenly, I focused momentarily on her instead of the road—to check if she was serious about this.

"You mean—the spot?"

She nodded. "Yes. I mean *the* spot."

Luce didn't need to tell me twice. I didn't expect much to happen; even if she wanted to sit in the truck and let me bask in her presence, I would've gladly accepted it and enjoyed it more than she knew. Our spot was in the southern part of the forest, in the middle of a few massive cedar trees that provided a perfect shield from curious eyes. Not that there were many there—especially not at this hour.

It felt as if my truck had bulldozed right through the forest to get to our spot before I parked it beneath 'our tree', one where our names were still carved, along with the date we first started dating. Over the years, I'd come here occasionally to stare at our initials and remember what we had together. I'd never come here with anyone else but her.

And I was about to voice that to her as I turned to face her, but before I could say a single word, her lips were against mine, and the world disappeared around us, as did any thought I had.

In an instant, she unbuckled her seatbelt and sat on my lap. I was particularly grateful for my truck's spaciousness at that moment since she could move around comfortably. My body followed its instincts, eager to have her as close to me as possible. I trailed my hands up her thighs, the thin fabric of her dress separating my eager fingertips from her exposed skin.

"Luce, fuck," I groaned as she ground herself against me, my cock growing hard in the restriction of my pants. She could sense it, too, because a small smirk crossed her face, and she only made her movements more intentional as her lips pressed against mine again.

"I want you to fuck me," she murmured, blending the words into our kiss. The directness of her statement floored me. Sure, we had slept together once before—after her return, and many things were said, but I figured that was 'in the heat of the moment' kind of a thing. But, hearing her say it now nearly made me lose my mind. My hand hiked up her dress, revealing more of her bare thighs that I caressed while she fiddled with my pants.

"Say it again," I demanded, my kiss a little rougher now as it traveled down her throat. Lucy tipped her head backward, her chest rising up and down rapidly with each heavy breath. It was mesmerizing to watch. When she finally managed to release my cock from my pants, she gave it one long stroke, causing my entire body to tense.

*This woman.*

"I want you inside me," she repeated herself, her hand inching down once more with each word. I didn't need more conviction than this. I wanted to be back inside her more than I wanted air. This time, I was ready regarding protection. It wasn't like I expected something to happen, but I wanted to make sure I was prepared if it did, so I had a few condoms in my wallet. I reached for it, retrieving one of the thin packages. I tore the plastic envelope and rolled the thin layer of protection over my cock. The moment I did, Luce pushed my hand out of the way. She moved her panties to the side, revealing her pussy that already glistened with sheer desire, and then she impaled herself on me.

I gripped her hips with a loud moan, tipping my head back as pleasure rushed through me. She was so warm and so fucking wet for me, and I was pretty sure this was the closest I would ever get to heaven.

"Fuck…Luce," I groaned again, as If I had suddenly lost the ability to speak, and this was the only thing I could think to say. I helped guide her pace as she moved on top of me in a slow, circular motion, massaging me from all angles. My gaze was locked on her beautiful face and how it crunched up with the bliss we shared. "Just like that. Ride my cock like a good girl you are." When I finally regained the ability to speak, all I wanted to do was praise her for how she moved on top of me.

"Luke…" she whimpered on top of me, gripping my shoulders to support herself further. My arms bracketed her slender body, drawing her in to remove any remaining free space between us. I couldn't allow it. Not now. Not ever again.

"I know, baby. I know," I hummed. The way her pussy tightened around me, letting me know just how good this felt for her. I dragged my lips to her chest, showering it in tender kisses, and tugging the delicate lace of her dress down ever-so-slightly to reveal more of her breasts. My brows furrowed as I realized she wasn't wearing a bra, and I looked up at her.

Still breathy, Luce allowed a smile to tug her lips upward. "This isn't the kind of a dress you can wear a bra with," she explained. *No complaints from me,* I thought to myself as I pulled her closer, burying my face back in her chest. I wanted to worship every inch of her.

Luce arched against me. Any teasing and playfulness that initially lingered between us was now long gone—neither of us could wait and play around any longer. Her pace on my lap became faster, harder, and more urgent as I held her close to me, feeling her pussy throb up around me more violently. My hands were shaking as they explored her body, overcame with the sweet adrenaline and pleasure.

"You feel good, so damn good," I praised her, unable to look away from her. It was as if somehow I had ended up inside a goddess—with how angelic she looked right then, there was no proof that wasn't the case in the first place.

"I'm close…I'm so damn close." Her words blended with another heavy moan, and that was my cue. My hand snuck in between her thighs, finding her tender, swollen clit, and rubbing it at a pace that followed her thrusts.

That did the trick it was meant to.

In only a few moments, Luce was tipped over the edge with a loud groan that echoed deep into the night as evidence of what happened here tonight. I would've been concerned someone had heard us in any other place, but here, it was just the two of us. She could scream as loud as she wanted. The juices of her arousal gushed all over me, soaking me in her pleasure, and that was my own undoing.

I tensed against her as I came, tightening my grip around her to hold her as close to me as possible. My lips eagerly crashed against hers to stifle the sounds that threatened to leave my throat, but it was pointless. The sensation that consumed me overpowered that attempt easily.

It took me a few moments to regain my composure and finally let her go. When I did, she remained on my lap, with my cock still inside her. Luce leaned her head against my shoulder, looking more content than ever. I basked in the sight, still unable to believe she was here…that she chose to be with me again. And while I didn't know what the future would bring for us, right now, this was enough.

"You know…there's a karaoke night that we're meant to go to," I pointed out after a few long moments of silence, even if that was the last thing I wanted to do. But, for her, I would. Luce didn't move, but I could practically feel her smile.

"Luke, I don't know how to tell you this…but we're not going anywhere unless you have a spare pair of pants in your truck. You're soaked." Mischief lingered on her expression as she looked up at me.

"And whose fault is that, huh?" I teased her, placing a soft kiss on her forehead. I traced lines over her back, content with just feeling the warmth of her body against mine. This was all I needed to be happy. "I just thought…you seemed very excited about the karaoke night, and I didn't want you to miss out on it. Even if I do think this was a much better use of our time."

Now, she laughed, and the melodic sound filled my truck. How I went without hearing it for ten years was now beyond me. I couldn't imagine living like that for another day. Deep in my heart, I knew I had to find a way to make this work because ever since that first kiss, there was no going back to how things used to be for me.

# Chapter 30
## Lucy

THINGS WERE LOOKING up in the best sense of those words. When I first arrived at Port-Cartier, I expected healing to be a more difficult process. I expected to be haunted by memories I spent so long running away from, to be tortured by my past, to be eager to return to Seattle and assure myself leaving was the best choice I ever made. And all my fears revolved around one person: Luke.

How ironic was that? The person I so feared to encounter, the person I left this town for, was now also the person who changed my life for the better—and most of my days passed without a single thought of Jason. Any wounds I had come here to heal were long forgotten; all I could think about was my future.

When I did think of it, it was by Luke's side.

"Hello? Earth to Luce!" Sailor called out on the other side of our video call. I had some floral arrangements to get through today, so I figured I could call my best friend and chat while doing it. The truth was, I missed her terribly. These past five weeks were the longest we had gone without seeing each other since we met. Only two more weeks were left of my supposed stay here, and I still hadn't made up my mind about what I was going to do. That was partially why I had been so silent today and why I called her to help.

"Sorry, I just have a lot on my mind right now," I mumbled, adding another lily to the arrangement I was working on. It was for the wedding of one of the girls I went to high school with, so I wanted to ensure everything was perfect. For the longest time, I thought marriage wasn't an option for me. It *definitely* wasn't when I was dating Jason. But with Luke... "I don't know what to do, Sailor. I've gotten myself in...this situation, and I don't know how to get out of it."

"You mean you and Luke?" She tilted her head to the side. I nodded. "Well, you do still have two weeks. Before you're meant to come back home. You will have to talk to him at some point..."

"I know, I know...I just...I can't ask him to leave the business he just bought from his father, but I'm also unsure where *I* belong. My life has been turned upside down. For the past decade, I have tried my best to stay as far away from this town as possible, afraid of the heartache it may trigger. But now that I'm back here, it feels like it's where I've belonged all along. It's the weirdest thing."

"First of all, you belong by my side. What kind of a question is that?" Sailor interrogated with a pouty expression on her face. I couldn't help but smile. "But, our friendship is so strong that it can take miles and miles of distance. If you ever look for a place where you belong, you will always find one by my side. With that said...if you're sure you're making the right decision, I'll support you if you decide to stay in Port-Cartier."

I rubbed my forehead. *That* was partially the issue. I wasn't sure if I could leave the life I had built in Seattle behind. What if I was about to make the biggest mistake of my life?

What if...

What if…

*What if…*

I hated those damn questions.

"The Sailor I know would never suggest I leave a life behind for a man," I pointed out teasingly. She rolled her eyes. "Who are you, and what have you done to my best friend?"

"Well, *this* Sailor can tell you're very much in love, Luce. And she only wants the best for you. If your heart is so torn about leaving…then leaving may not be the best choice after all."

"I know, but—"

"And you can always try long distance. I mean, what's the rush? You can travel back and forth, and so can he. There is no reason either of you should leave your life behind for now, right? And if you do it for, say, a year, then I think you'll have a much clearer answer on the right move."

Some of the tension in my shoulders practically vanished at her words. I had been so stuck with mulling this over that I forgot it was possible to meet in the middle. "That…may be a good idea." It wasn't ideal, of course, but it was the closest to the optimal solution we'd come up with. At least until more answers crystalized in our minds. "I mean, I don't want to spend much time away from him, but what can I do?"

Sailor gave me a sympathetic look because we both knew this was as good as it could get. "It will be okay. You're one of the most resourceful and capable people I have ever met, and I don't doubt you'll figure this all out. At one point, you'll know what's right, and you'll go for it. Because that's the kind of person *my* Lucy is."

A warmth spread through me in an instant. She often gave me more credit than I deserved, but I felt invincible with her by my side. If there was one person I could always count on to make me feel better, it was her. Fate must have brought us together for moments like this when we stood by each other and helped make impossible situations a little more possible.

"How's Eve doing, by the way? Still stuck at home?" she swiftly changed the topic, which I greatly appreciated.

"Unfortunately. Her doctor says she'll be out for at least a few more weeks before she can even *attempt* to work part-time. Her recovery is going well, but she'll need time. I think the fact that she can still be useful from the house is making it easier for her. She's always been a workaholic."

"Sounds like someone else I know," Sailor interrupted me. I rolled my eyes.

"Right now, I don't have a choice. I want everything to be set up for my mom once she can return to work. The software and her POS system are set up. I'm making a few more adjustments in her system, which should be it..." I was determined to prepare everything for my mom's return. Everything aside from one—and perhaps the most important—thing.

"What about a new employee? I mean, what's going to happen once you leave? If your mom still can't work..."

Within the next two weeks, while I was still in Port-Cartier, I had to find another worker for my mom's business. A part of me refused to find someone already because giving this position to someone else felt definitive, and I wasn't ready for that yet. This town was filled with good people who poured their hearts into everything they did, but I also couldn't help but feel that none of them would be good enough for the job. But that was a worry for another day. Today, I had to sort out the floral arrangements before me.

"I guess I'll cross that bridge when I get to it. I've gotten some applications, but honestly, I haven't taken a look at them yet..."

"Is there a reason?" Sailor questioned me.

My heart twisted in my chest as I pondered my response. For

the first time in forever, I couldn't bring myself to be honest with Sailor. "I've just been swamped," I said softly. "Thank you—for all of this. I legitimately don't know what I would do without you. But I really need to get these sorted out"—I gestured at the flowers in front of me—"and you keep distracting me!"

"You're the one who called *me*!" she retorted, waving her finger at me through the screen. Chuckles broke out from both our mouths, and for a split second, life really wasn't that complicated. "Without me, you'd be far lonelier and laughing less. Anyway, I love you, girl. I'll talk to you soon. And don't you worry; you'll figure it all out. What's meant to be will find a way, and the more I hear you talk about Luke, the more I'm sure this is meant to be."

"I love you too. And thank you. Again." I couldn't say it enough.

Just as Sailor hung up—almost on cue—the front doorbell rang, and Luke entered the flower store. A smile was plastered across his face—the kind that made my heart yearn for more of his presence.

"Welcome to Blushing Blooms. What can I do for you today?" I teased him as he approached my counter. His smile widened.

"Well, I'm looking for someone to bring to my family's BBQ this Sunday." He arched his brow. "If you know someone, I'd be thankful if you'd let me know."

"Hmm…" I hummed as I approached him, wrapping my arms around his neck. Luke leaned in, kissing my lips softly. The butterflies fluttered in my stomach like they did all those years ago. It was the feeling I remembered so vividly over the years—the feeling I thought I would never experience again. "Well, I'll have to check my schedule, but I may be available to join you."

"Wonderful," Luke responded, keeping his hands on my hips. "You know, you've been missed on these BBQs over the years. My family tried not to mention you because they saw the breakup wasn't easy for me either—"

"Then you shouldn't have broken up with me," I pointed out.

Luke rolled his eyes before he continued, "But every now and then, your name would pop up. As it should have. You've always been a part of my family." I felt the same way. We had been together for years and were friends for even longer beforehand. And while our past could never be changed, our future could. And I looked forward to building it with him.

"We're older now. We have to do better. No more secret schemes and no more lies." My eyes locked on his, noting the everlasting softness that resided there. The more I stared at him, the more I realized how much I searched for him in every man I dated over the past ten years. But no one could ever compare—because they weren't Luke.

"I promise. I'd be an idiot ever to let you go again. Whether you like it or not, you really are stuck with me…"

While we both wanted to enjoy this piece of heaven for a little longer, I knew we had to discuss what was going to happen once these last two weeks were up. And we needed to be realistic. Neither of us could allow ourselves to lose our jobs.

"There's nothing I'd like more," I admitted, finally prying myself away from his warm embrace. "But we do need to discuss what we're going to do. I'm only staying for two more weeks, and then I have to return to my job."

I had some savings, but working at my mom's place would be a financial hit. She loved her flower shop, and people who lived here loved it as well, but the truth was, her prices were far too low and barely making any profit for her, let alone the two of us. And I truly did love teaching, even if it wasn't the path I originally planned.

"That's easy," Luke said calmly. "I'll follow you in Seattle."

"Luke, you can't just follow me in Seattle. We've only reunited weeks ago. This may very well be a honeymoon phase. I don't want you to do something you'll regret—"

He pressed his index fingers against my lips to silence all my concerns. Rolling my eyes, I swatted his hand away from my mouth.

"First, we're not just in the 'honeymoon' phase. From the moment I first met you, I knew you were the one for me. We've spent the past ten years away from each other, but I've only been more sure of it in your absence," he explained. The fluttering sensation in my stomach returned, but I tried to chase it away. I needed to stay focused. "And I'd never regret coming with you. You know what I do regret? Letting you go all those years ago. I meant it when I said it, Luce. I'd be a fool to let you go again. I'm never making that mistake again. You're the best damn thing to have ever happened to me."

"Now you're just trying to sweet-talk me into that BBQ..." I crossed my arms over my chest, still keeping that teasing tone in my voice. Luke laughed, sending a wave of tingles through my body.

"I thought that was a done deal kind of thing?" His brows shot up.

"I have to make you work for it—if even just a little bit." I leaned back against my counter. "Anyway, I talked to Sailor." Luke arched his brow, so I quickly explained, "My best friend, remember?"

He nodded. I couldn't blame him. That aspect of my life still remained an enigma to him, but I looked forward to introducing him to the life I had built in Seattle soon. "Right."

"And she suggested that we could do a long-distance thing for a while. I mean, I've been so stressed out about how this will work that I didn't even think that was an option..." I expected to see the same relief I felt when Sailor first suggested it, but Luke's expression didn't yield. He didn't even have to say it; I knew he wasn't sold on the idea. "You don't think that's going to work?"

"I think...I'll do whatever you want me to. I'm committed to this—to us. But I can't lie and say that a long-distance relationship will be easy. It won't. I've spent so many years away from you, and the thought of having to spend even a single second away from you all over again is enough to drive me insane." He stepped forward, trailing his fingers down my arm. "And while I'm not overly fond of it and would much rather follow you to the end of the world if this is what you think is the best for us, I'll do it. Because it's about both of us now. I promise never to make a decision that impacts us both on my own as I did all those years ago."

I squinted my eyes. "Who are you, and what have you done to my Luke? Had you appeared a little sooner, all of this would've been much simpler..."

Again, his laugh spread through the flower shop like wildfire. It was infectious. "I'm still your Luke, baby, only now, I'm more in love than ever."

# Chapter 31
## Luke



WITH LUCE'S hand in mine, we headed to the weekly Sunday BBQ. It felt like I had somehow returned to the past and been given a second chance, and I had every intention of using every second of it.

Luce had suggested a long-distance relationship. I had heard many horror stories about them that I didn't want to bring up with her, especially since she seemed so relieved when she laid the plan out for me. We were both committed to making this work, and I *tried* to keep Landon's words in my mind. I couldn't scare her off by moving too fast or enforcing my strong wishes to always be with her. I waited for ten years…surely, I could wait a little more.

Still, one of the things I would miss was lunches like this all over again. Luce seemed particularly stiff as we stood before my parents' home, and I couldn't quite tell why. She looked as beautiful as ever in a white shirt and jean shorts, with her hair braided to be kept out of her face. Her knuckles whitened as she insisted on bringing in a six-pack of my family's favorite beer.

"Are you sure you don't want me to take that beer from you?"

"I'm sure," she said, "I want to make a good first impression."

*Good first impression?* My brows furrowed. Had I somehow entered an alternate dimension where she hadn't met my family yet?

"What are you talking about, Luce? My family knows you, and they adore you. I thought that much was obvious from when they came to help prepare your home for your mom. Not to mention all the times you've been here a decade ago."

"No, I know, it's just..." She pressed her lips into a thin line. "It's been a long time. I've changed since the last time they've seen me. And when they came to help, the focus was on the house and my mom. And we weren't dating yet. Today, the focus *will* probably be on us. And I'm just...nervous."

Though she elaborated on her train of thought, it still made little sense to me. Luce was loved by all those around her, and *especially* my parents and brothers. Even having a passing thought that may not be the case was ridiculous.

I turned to face her, cupping her cheeks with my hands. The motion brought an odd sense of deja vu. We had stood here many times before when we were teenagers, always somehow entrapping ourselves in a meaningful conversation at my parents' doorstep. I suppose some things never changed.

"Don't be silly. They'll love you as much as I love you..." The words made such a subtle appearance and slipped from my mouth so effortlessly that I didn't even realize it until it was too late. This went against the advice Landon had given me, so I quickly did some damage control by leaning in and pressing my lips against hers, hoping the kiss would somehow make her forget that I just said 'I love you' in this phase of our lives.

I also hoped it would soothe my mind because she didn't say it back.

The door flung open then, and Logan's annoying face popped up with a cheeky grin. "You know, if you two need a room, there's one available upstairs..." he commented jokingly as we pulled back from each other.

"No need for a room, though I do need a fridge," Luce countered quickly, holding up the six-pack. It appeared to work like a charm because Logan instantly dragged her in, shouting.

"Mom! They're here! And Luce brought beer!"

My mom rushed out of the kitchen with the broadest smile. Like the rest of my family, she was genuinely delighted to see Luce.

"My sweet darling girl," she said as Luce pulled her into a tight hug. I smiled at the sight. If this didn't convince her that my family loved her just the same, I didn't know what would. "I'm so glad you're back with Luke. That boy has been a mess since you two broke up"—my mom shot me a stern glance—"and that has entirely been *his* fault."

I threw my hands up defensively to show I meant no harm. "I'm standing right here, you know."

My dad and Landon came from the porch to greet her as well, embracing her tightly and showing how they felt about all of this.

"You've been missed, Luce." Landon gave her a small pat on the back. "Mom's right. Someone has to keep Luke on the leash a little bit..."

"*Hey!*" I interrupted them, only to earn a small chuckle from Luce. They could have teased me all they wanted at that moment if it meant hearing that sound again.

"Why don't you come join me in the kitchen? I need some help with the salad, and we have so much to catch up on," Mom said as she hooked her arm around Luce's. Luce seemed much more relaxed now that she had seen things hadn't changed. She was just as important to us now as she was all those years ago—especially me.

I knew it was *far* too soon, and we had a lot to figure out, but I knew she was the love of my life and the woman I would spend the rest of my life with. So, it was only natural that the thought of marriage crossed my mind more times than I wanted to admit.

A firm pat on my back interrupted me from daydreaming about Lucy in a wedding dress, and I looked up at Landon, who had a knowing glint in his eyes. He was the oldest and claimed to be the wisest. We often challenged him on it, but maybe there was some truth to his words.

"You've done something, haven't you?" he commented. I desperately wanted to say no and pretend I could follow his advice, but it wasn't like me to lie to my brothers. On the other hand, it was a different story to lie *for* my brothers. My parents could confirm it.

"I told her I loved her just before we entered the house. And I've also been standing here and thinking about the day I marry her."

Landon's face scrunched slightly. Whatever first came to his mind, he somehow resisted saying it out loud. "I see." He stroked his neatly trimmed stubble. "I do think you have some things to figure out before the marriage part, brother."

"I know," I assured him, staring at the sight of Luce in the kitchen. The wall blocked most of my view, so I could only see her arm and a part of her ass, but the sight was just as mesmerizing. Especially paired with her angelic laughter. "But I also know I will marry her someday. So, whatever we have to figure out along the way, we will."

The BBQ preparations took a good forty-five minutes before we were all ready and seated at the wooden table on our back porch. Lucy sat beside me, and she hadn't stopped smiling for the past ten minutes as she entered the wooden porch. On the other hand, I was sent down a spiral, where all I could think about was the day she'd become my wife and the mother of my children. Someday, they would join us on this porch for our Sunday lunch tradition.

"So, Luce, how long are you staying here? Is your mom doing better?" my dad asked after lengthy praise of his BBQ skills. He had put a lot of effort into the lunch today since Luce was joining us.

She took a sip of her beer, looking at me momentarily before her eyes set on my dad. Her sweet scent of vanilla mixed with coconut hit my nostrils, and I was pretty sure it sent me into some frenzy where all I could think about was her. This wasn't normal. I was so in love with her it felt like that love may burst out of me at any point now.

"Well, I'm not sure yet. I do work as a teacher, so I'll have to go back for the school year…" she explained. I bracketed my arm around her, trailing lines up and down her arm. "And my mom is doing better. She's still restless, but I'm keeping her confined to the house."

Landon gave his nod of approval. "That's good. Rest is crucial at the early stages of recovery, and while it may seem like a long time to your mom…in the long run, it really hasn't been that long. I'll do a home visit to check on her next week."

"Thank you. I can't thank you enough for everything you've done for her," Luce said softly. Logan rolled his eyes, giving Landon a big pat on the shoulder.

"It's his job, Luce. Don't you worry."

"A teacher, you say?" my mom asked curiously like she hadn't discussed what Lucy did for living with Eve a hundred times. She also likely wanted to steer the conversation in a different direction before it was too late. "I never thought you'd become a teacher, from what I can remember..."

"Well, a lot has changed since then. I didn't expect teaching to be my life's calling, but I'm pleasantly surprised with how my career has worked out. I do genuinely enjoy working with kids, and I hope to be able to do that for a long time."

"It'd be good to have someone like you 'round here, girl," my father commented. He took a big swing of his beer. Ever since his retirement, he had developed a particular interest in beer and considered himself somewhat of a guru. On the other hand, we thought he only utilized that title to have a cold beer on hot summer days. "We've had a shortage of teachers for a while now. It's been tough."

"I know. Mrs. Fairmont had mentioned it when she stopped by the flower shop," Luce replied. "I'm truly sorry to hear it. You'd think people would give anything to come to a town like this..."

"Well, that is usually the case during the tourist season," my dad said, grabbing himself some ribs. "But the rest of the year, I can't say it's been great. Surely, your mom has mentioned it to you, too."

One look at her face told me everything I needed to know. Luce didn't know how much the town had to change over the years, and her mom didn't want to make her feel bad. It wasn't horrible by any means, but it could always be better—particularly in the education department.

"Luce has made incredible changes at the Blushing Blooms, so you better believe that place is going to blossom even more," I said. Lucy's lips twitched as if she was trying to hold back a smile.

"God, you're lame," Logan commented, "especially now that your girlfriend is here."

Despite his comment, my family dug into the food. I had warned them before not to discuss how our relationship was going to work after these next two weeks since I didn't want to overwhelm her. I had likely managed to do that on my own by prematurely admitting my feelings. I knew she was aware of how I felt about her, but saying it out loud was a different thing entirely.

"I must say, Levi, retirement looks good on you," Luce continued the conversation after Logan's brief teasing crusade. "It's been well-deserved after all those years of hard work."

My mom shook her head, extending her hand to my dad's stomach and patting it lightly.

"Oh, Luce, he's about one beer away from a retirement beer belly. Don't flatter him too much." Despite her teasing comment, so much love and affection was held in her tone—so openly displayed for everyone to see. I was lucky enough to have grown up in a family with happy parents who loved each other and gave me a perfect example of the father and husband I need to become one day. And finally, after so many years spent alone, it felt like that day may come soon.

The rest of the BBQ continued in a cheerful tone, with a wide display of different meats and side dishes that my parents had put together. Mom had even made a cake. Not a single second of this meal passed where I wasn't thankful for everything I had in my arm's reach, right up to the moment when we were supposed to leave.

My parents escorted us to the front porch, and both of them made it a point to give Lucy a big hug.

"You're welcome here anytime, sweetheart," my mom told her. "I hope you know that."

"I know," my girl responded. "Look, Levi, Linda…I can't thank you enough for everything you've done for me. Both ten years ago and when my mom got home from the hospital." Her teeth momentarily sunk into her bottom lip, like she was trying to stop it from quivering. My hand found the small of her back, giving her the reassurance to continue. "I know I disappeared all those years ago without a goodbye, and I can't tell you how much I've regretted it ever since…I just—"

"Oh, darling," Mom said quickly, pulling her in another hug. I felt the back of my eyes burn, too, but I tried to keep it under control. I hated that she was the one apologizing for something I had done. I was the one to break us up. "You have nothing to apologize for. Family will always be family, no matter how hard some of our choices are."

"And you better believe you've been a part of our family ever since that boy," my dad said as he gestured toward me, "first brought you to our doorstep to introduce you as his girlfriend."

Luce nodded, but no other word made it past her lips. I linked my hand with hers and took over our goodbye.

"Thanks for a good BBQ. Dad, you've truly outdone yourself this time around," I pointed out, trying to lighten the moon. Mom huffed, waving her hand at us.

"You boys…always stroking each other's egos…" she grumbled before she headed back inside with my dad. My focus was now entirely on Lucy, who still looked like something was on her mind. "Are you all right?"

She nodded. "Sorry, I just…I just had this moment of guilt overcome me. When I left, I didn't even consider how it may affect those around me. At the very least, I should have said goodbye or explained myself."

"Hey." I grasped her chin between my fingers, tilting her head so our gazes met. "You have nothing to apologize for. I was the one who broke your heart, and everything you've done, you've done to deal with that pain. If you want someone to blame, I'm right here…"

Finally, a smile lit up her face. "I don't want to blame anyone. Not anymore. But I do want to have a karaoke night…" I let out a small groan, leaning down and kissing her lips regardless.

"If I remember correctly, you were the one to disrupt the karaoke night the last time we were supposed to attend one..." I trailed off, pecking her lips again. "Are you sure you'll behave this time around?"

"Perhaps." A mischievous glint lingered in her eyes. "You may want to take me home first so I can get that out of my system first, and then we'll do the karaoke..." Grasping her in my arms, I carried her over to my truck. A slight squeal accompanied each step on her end. If it meant spending the rest of my life by her side, I'd gladly have karaoke night every night.

# Chapter 32
## Lucy

MY EXCITEMENT WAS hard to contain as I stretched out in Luke's bed. We *were* meant to do karaoke last night, but I found out I would rather spend my time tangled up in his bedsheets instead of singing my favorite songs in the bar.

Maybe a day would come when I would finally get used to all of this—but it hadn't happened *yet*. And I wanted to spend as much time with him as possible.

To make up for another missed karaoke night, Luke promised to take me somewhere special today. But first, I had to head back home to change because there was no way I was going anywhere in one of my casual outfits, which were reserved for family and friends only.

Luke's arm draped over me as he pulled me closer to his bare body, showering my shoulder with soft kisses.

"Good morning," he said, his tone low and hoarse. "How'd you sleep?"

I looked back at him over my shoulder. "Amazing," I admitted, "this bed is divine."

Luke chuckled, leaning over to kiss me. For the past few weeks, I had received countless kisses. It'd usually annoy me with any of my ex-boyfriends, but with Luke, I couldn't get enough of it. Maybe it was because I constantly felt like I was running out of time. Or perhaps it was just the effect he had on me. I couldn't tell. Either way, I wasn't going to complain.

"You're more than welcome to stay in it whenever you'd like," he assured me, pushing his body against mine. I could already feel him harden behind me, and, as much as I wanted to feel him inside of me again, I was in a more teasing mood today. Grabbing the sheets, I pulled them around my body as I sat up, looking back at him.

"I will take your offer into consideration, but for now...I need to shower and head back home to check on my mom and change my clothes. You have something special planned today, don't you?"

"A gentleman doesn't kiss and tell, though the temptation is strong in your presence..." He trailed off. I stood up, still keeping that cheeky smile on my face. I couldn't remember the last time I felt this comfortable in someone's presence. For years, I had always kept my guard up and been careful not to open up too much. I knew, better than anyone, how easy it was for all of it to fall apart and for your heart to get broken.

And now, ironically enough, my first and biggest heartbreak was mending all the broken parts of me.

"If any gentlemen were present in this room, I'd invite them to join me in the shower..." I backed into the bathroom, dropping the sheets on my way there and soaking in the way Luke's gaze washed over me. He was out of bed in a heartbeat and chased me into the bathroom. He started the shower, which quickly filled the bathroom with steam as we stepped in.

"There may be a gentleman present here," Luke told me, his gaze darkening. My knees were weak at the sight, and I couldn't wait to have him closer. Any of my intentions to tease him had dispersed in a heartbeat. "But there will be nothing gentleman-like in the way I'll get on my knees for you."

I thought he was joking. That was who Luke was—always teasing and joking with others. But nothing was teasing in how he looked at me as he did, indeed, get on his knees before me. His eyes were filled with the most primal lust that had every part of my body reacting, already building up with sweet anticipation.

"Luke..." was all I managed to muster before he leaned forward, resting one of his hands on my hip while the other instinctively found my entrance. He pressed his lips against my pussy, sticking his tongue out to move in one long stroke that brushed against all the right places. I tipped my head back, knotting my fingers in his hair as if it would help me anchor myself through the following sensation. He felt so good against my pussy; I wasn't even sure how such an intense bliss could be real. My legs were already trembling, and he had only just begun. He knew exactly how my body responded to him even after all of these years.

"Oh, God..." I whimpered, rolling my hips forward to take more of what he had to offer. I closed my eyes, with hot water rolling down my bare body as he took me with his fingers and his mouth.

And while I fought through the haze of pleasure, one thing popped into my mind.

Could I go on without this again?

After our shower, which took much longer than expected, we returned to my mom's house. Before we left for whatever Luke had planned, I wanted to make sure she was fine, and that Ed could check in on her in case she needed anything. And I needed something other than a white top and jean shorts to wear.

As Luke's truck approached my childhood home, my gaze was instantly drawn to an unfamiliar car. My heart dropped to my stomach, and the worst possible scenarios roamed in my mind right away. Did something happen to my mom?

*God, I'll never forgive myself if she got hurt again and I wasn't there,* I frantically thought.

"Luce…" Luke called out, but his voice was a silent echo. He had barely pulled his truck up, and I had already hopped out of the door and ran towards the front porch. My heart raced wildly in my chest, threatening to shatter into a million pieces at any point.

*Please, be okay,* I silently pleaded. Things had just started looking up, and I couldn't handle even just the thought of everything falling apart again. My eyes started to well up as I slowed down, only for my gaze to set on a familiar figure.

"Jason?" I called out, just to make sure. It couldn't be him. What kind of a fever dream would I have to be trapped in for him to actually come to Port-Cartier?

When he turned around, my worst suspicions had been brought to life. He was dressed in his usual attire—sweatpants and a white T-shirt, though his hair and stubble were long overdue for some trimming.

"Luce…" He exhaled in relief. Behind me, Luke had caught up with my steps and was now standing by my side. My mom was fine, thankfully, but I was about to have a very uncomfortable encounter.

"What the hell are you doing here?" The words slipped from my lips before I could think them through. I couldn't believe his audacity. Not only had he cheated, but he also had the balls to show up here for whatever ridiculous reason he had scrambled up in his mind. "Did Sarah come to visit, too?"

Jason's eyes darted between Luke and me. I figured he was wondering who Luke was—if it was the same guy he heard over the phone. I decided it was none of his damn business.

"Sarah and I broke up. That's why I'm here. I fucked up. Massively. I know it. But that mistake made me realize how much I care about you. How much I need you in my life. Nothing has been the same since you left…and now I see what I lost. So, I've come here to fix my mistakes and beg you to come back home to me."

"You're in for a rough awakening, buddy," Luke said beside me. I appreciated that he didn't try to intervene—too much, at least. "She's not coming back home to you."

"Who the fuck are you? This is between Luce and me," Jason challenged him, stepping forward. The way his testosterone could rise in a matter of seconds was one of his most unattractive flaws. A few words were all it took for him to try to start a fight. Luke remained calm beside me.

"I'm Lucy's boyfriend," he said coldly. His hand rested on my back. "And I suggest you get in your car and leave before things get ugly."

Jason laughed, but it was the manic kind in the most unstable way, prompting me to take a step back. I was thankful Luke was by my side if things took a turn for the worse.

"She wouldn't move on from me so quickly. We have a life together—an apartment. And we were happy. This was just a bump on the road, but I'm here to fix all of it." Now, his eyes locked on mine. "I'm not letting you go. I can't. I love you. You're the best thing that has ever happened to me."

Months ago, I would've given anything to hear those words from him. Now, they didn't affect me in any way, shape or form. I just wanted him gone so I could go on with my life. "We had a life together. But you messed it up and—"

"Because you were distant! Because that's what you do. You get distant when things get real!"

My expression scrunched in confusion. I thought he would've gotten more rise out of me. If Sailor had been here, she likely would've punched him. But I was…oddly calm.

"Jason," I said, my tone more serious now. "Really, I appreciate you coming all the way out here, but I'm not interested in working things out with you. I'm happy with my life as it is." The heartbreak on his face deepened with each word that left my mouth. "I'm not coming back. I don't love you anymore." I wasn't sure I ever did. Not in the way I loved Luke.

"But you got my flowers...and my note. I explained myself in the note," he insisted. "Haven't you seen it? It all makes sense..."

"I never read the note. There wasn't any need to because my mind was made. I'm not going back. What's done is done. And really, I wish you all the best...as long as it's far away from me." I could honestly tell him that. After so much pain and hurt, I was healed and genuinely wanted him to live the best life possible. Life finally felt good, and I wasn't about to jeopardize that in any way. Luke lowered his hand, and I gently let my fingers find his. None of this healing would've been possible without him.

Jason scoffed, shaking his head. "I see now it was a mistake to come here...to think you'd actually want to fix something once in your life. You're the cold, distant bi—"

Before he could finish the words, Luke released my hand and took a few threatening steps forward. He towered over Jason, his posture tense.

"You better fucking think twice about finishing that sentence," he warned Jason. Luke didn't swear often, so his words carried additional weight. Not that Jason knew it. "I won't tolerate you speaking that way about her. I suggest you leave."

Jason didn't budge. Instead, he continued to stare at Luke with that same daring look. "You think you know her, but I promise you, you don't." Jason finally stepped back. "She's only going to fuck you up. But, by the time you realize it, it will be too late. So, good luck to you, and don't say I didn't warn you."

Jason pushed past Luke, heading straight to his sports car. He started the engine with a roar and then sped down the street. Just like that, he was out of my life...hopefully, for good. I watched the empty street for a moment longer, still trying to comprehend what just happened before I finally turned to Luke.

When I did, something was different in his eyes. I couldn't figure out what it was, but it terrified me.

"Luke?" I questioned softly, looking for an explanation for his demeanor change.

"Flowers and notes, Luce? And you didn't think to tell me about any of it?" His voice radiated hurt that I wanted to soothe more than anything else. The flowers and the note had been so damn irrelevant that I didn't give them a second thought, but I could see how it may come across to Luke.

*Like I was hiding something.*

"I didn't care about the flowers or the note, so I didn't mention them. I only want to be with you, and I—"

"Luce, stop," he interrupted me, his tone pained. I fell silent, staring at him. This wasn't how today was supposed to go. We were supposed to have fun—and I planned to tell him that I had made my decision about what I wanted to do. But now, it had all gone to hell. If I told him my plan now, it would've seemed like I was trying to find my way out of an uncomfortable situation.

"I mean it. It didn't matter to me. That's why I didn't bring it up."

"That's not the point." Luke rubbed his forehead. "Let's just take a few hours away from each other to process all of this and think about what we will do. I don't want either of us to make rash decisions or say something we will regret later." The burning behind my eyes had intensified. If we couldn't get through this, how would we get through anything else life threw at us? We were supposed to be a team, but right now, it couldn't feel further away than that. With nothing else to say, I nodded.

"Fine. We'll talk later," was all I managed to say as I turned on my heels and rushed into my home. The last thing I wanted was for him to see the tear that rolled down my cheek.

# Chapter 33
## Luke

**WHAT THE HELL** *had I done?*

Only an hour had passed since I left Luce at her home, yet my mind continued to reel, with a spreading suspicion in the pit of my stomach. I fucked up. With each moment that ticked away, I was more than sure of it.

I had spent the past ten years craving her presence, wishing I hadn't let her go that day. The thoughts of what I could have done differently haunted me for years, and now that I had a chance to make things right, I was messing them up all over again.

Without a moment of hesitation, I started my truck. It had been parked at our spot in the forest, where I often came to clear my mind. I had spent an hour blankly staring at the two initials carved into the bark, surrounded by a heart I *tried* to do myself.

*"What are you doing, Luke?" Luce couldn't stop laughing as she watched me carve into the bark. It wasn't my fault; the bark was the problem. It was unusually hard and uneven. This wasn't my first rodeo, so I knew something was up with this tree. I practiced this before to impress her—not that I'd say it out loud.*

*But no matter how hard I tried to explain the logistics to her, she didn't believe me. "That doesn't even look like a heart. Well, maybe if I squint my eyes..."*

*Now, I couldn't help but smile either. I looked back at her, unable to believe how lucky I was to have a girl like her with me.*

*"I'm purposely making it uneven like that," I told her, "to show that even when things aren't perfect, we'll stick together."*

The view of the uneven heart did the trick—I knew what I had to do.

I had to make things right and tell her how I felt. I didn't want to spend another second away from her; I wanted to hold her in my arms and assure her everything would be okay.

I meant it when I said it. I was all in, and it was time to prove it.

The drive to her home passed in the blink of an eye with how focused my mind was on what needed to be said and done. My body was on autopilot, moving between the streets with muscle memory that took over the charge of my truck. My head was elsewhere, and my heart was aching to see her and apologize.

When I finally pulled up in front of her home, I didn't head for the front door. Instead, I hopped over the fence and moved into the backyard. It was still perfectly maintained. I guessed that was Ed's doing while Eve was unable to do it.

I swept my hand over the ground until I found the tiniest rock I could spot. With great precision, I tossed it on the familiar window on the second floor. I had done this dozens of times a decade ago, and my precision remained intact. It was like riding a bike.

A few seconds passed before Luce opened the window and stared at me. Her brows furrowed in confusion, and her eyes were red from crying.

*Fuck.*

"What are you doing here?" she asked, her tone quiet as

she leaned against her window's white, wooden frame. "I thought you wanted some time to—"

"Fuck that," I said. "I want to talk to you. I don't want to spend another second away from you…" I hesitated. "If you'll still have me, of course. Can I come in?"

"You know, there's this thing we call front door that people use nowadays when they want to enter someone's home…" Luce retorted. *Good*, I thought to myself. If she was joking, that meant I hadn't *entirely* fucked up.

"And where's the fun in that?" I sized up the tree. The lowest branch was still within my reach, though I was much heavier than I was in my teenage years. I leaped and grabbed hold of the branch, pulling myself up. I took a moment before climbing my way up on some thinner branches that threatened to crack under my build.

"If you fall, I'm calling Landon, and you'll have to explain what you were doing…" she called out, watching me.

"If that happens, please, just let me die in peace." I finally reached the branch that was close to her window. I reached out and swung myself over the windowsill, landing right before her.

"No dying today, I see," Luce stated, crossing her arms over her chest. The moment I was on my feet, I stepped toward her.

"I'm sorry. That's the first thing you need to know. I'm so sorry. I don't know why I got so fired up over those flowers and the note. Why I didn't hear you out." I exhaled, running my hand through my hair. "Well, actually, maybe I do. I got upset because you'll be leaving soon, Luce. Once you're gone and back to the life you've built in Seattle, I'm terrified that you'll realize there may not be a spot for me there after all. Maybe it will be too much. Maybe you'll need—"

"Luke."

Now, I was pacing around her bedroom. It looked just like it did ten years ago, almost as if it had somehow been frozen in time. It was both impressive and creepy at the same time. "No, I need to say this. Please. I'm terrified that we won't be able to handle the distance. Because it will be hard, and I love you too damn much to be selfish. I can't even—"

"I love you too," she interrupted me again, and this time, the world stilled around me. In fact, I was pretty sure my breath had been sucked from my lungs. "You don't need to worry about long distance. I'm not going anywhere. I decided I want to stay in Port-Cartier."

That was it. There was no way this was happening. I had likely fallen from the tree and somehow ended up in a coma —that was the only logical explanation I could think of for the words that she had just said.

"What?" I stammered in disbelief. "But you love your job. I don't want you to sacrifice anything in your life."

"I do love my job, but I have a meeting scheduled with the principal of the elementary school to interview for a position." She extended her hand toward me, and I took it, still trying to understand what was happening. Hallucinations were another possibility… "I ran as far as I could when I left this town ten years ago. So much so that I had forgotten all about its magic. I have never been able to make a home out of another town, and now I know why. It's because the home has been waiting for me here all along, right by your side."

I closed the distance between us in one short step, and my lips collided against hers. She was right. By each other's side, we had everything we'd ever need. My body was overwhelmed with so many different emotions, but the most prominent one was relief because I got to keep my girl by my side.

"I love you," I repeated the words again. It was the only sentence that could snap through the synapses of my brain and make it to my lips.

"I love you, too," Luce whispered in return. Four simple words and an eternity before us to get to hear them.

. . .

Want more of Luke and Lucy's story?
Preorder Christmas Promises coming out November 14th.

After ten years apart, Luke and Lucy are finally spending their first Christmas together. The occasion is already joyous, but Luke is determined to make it the most special year ever. And he has come up with a plan to make it happen.

For the next twelve days, he will give Lucy a present each day. Some will remind them of the past they share, while others will help them build new memories together. Either way, he intends to cherish every moment they spend by each other's side.

His plan includes a few key things: gathering the entire family, flying Lucy's best friend to Port-Cartier, and finding the perfect ring to symbolize the start of a new chapter in their lives together. But, by the time Christmas rolls around, Lucy has a surprise of her own to share.

# acknowledgments

First, I just want to say thank you for reading this book. This story has been living in my head for years and I am so glad to finally be able to share it with you. These characters are like my babies. I hope you loved them as much as I loved writing them. I can't wait to share Logan and Landon's stories with you. There may even be a spin-off planned! If you haven't done so already, please consider leaving a review. It helps more than you know.

I had so much support writing this book. It wouldn't have been possible without the help from the people below.

Eric, thank you for being my inspiration behind Luke. You hold me up when I need the support and are one of my loudest cheerleaders. This writing journey wouldn't be possible without you.

To my boys, Harry and Charlie, you two are the best things ever to happen to me. I love how supportive you are of mom's dream and how excited you both get when I show you my books. Keep being awesome little dudes.

To my family, thank you for how supportive you were when I showed you my first book. You instantly read it and proceeded to ask when the next book was coming out. Thank you for supporting my dream.

To DerpyWickedFox Editorial, thank you for polishing this book and making it shine.

To Florence and the whole team at Happily Booked PR, I couldn't have done this without you. Thank you for helping me to promote my books.

To Aida at Algart, thank you for making the most beautiful cover and perfectly capturing Lucy and Luke.

To Sara at Sara's Design Services, thank you for making the formatting this book and being so excited when I told you about Broken Promises.

Finally, thank you to the bookish community. I have made some amazing friends and I could not be more thankful for the people I have met there. You have welcomed me with open arms.

# also by mia elliot

<u>Twisted by Tarot Series</u>

The Wheel of Fate

# about the author

Growing up in a small town in Maine, Mia's childhood was full of countless books filled with love stories, adventure, mystery, and, at times, magic. Her love for these tales grew into a passion for story-telling and filling uncounted notebook pages with vibrant characters.

Through the busyness and stresses of life, Mia always returns to her characters and imagined places, keeping writing as her passion and her outlet to unwind, recharge, and recenter. She currently lives in Maine with her husband and two boys.